About the Author

DM Binelli enchants readers with magical tales that seamlessly weave real-life inspiration into uplifting fantasies. His stories radiate a feel-good glow, offering readers a delightful escape into a world where joy and positivity prevail.

John Ryder and the Incredible Golden Pond

D. M. Binelli

John Ryder and the Incredible Golden Pond

Olympia Publishers
London

www.olympiapublishers.com
OLYMPIA PAPERBACK EDITION

Copyright © D. M. Binelli 2024

The right of D. M. Binelli to be identified as the author of
this work has been asserted in accordance with sections 77 and 78 of
the Copyright, Designs and Patents Act 1988.

All Rights Reserved

No reproduction, copy or transmission of this publication
may be made without written permission.
No paragraph of this publication may be reproduced,
copied or transmitted save with the written permission of the publisher,
or in accordance with the provisions
of the Copyright Act 1956 (as amended).

Any person who commits any unauthorised act in relation to
this publication may be liable to criminal
prosecution and civil claims for damage.

A CIP catalogue record for this title is
available from the British Library.

ISBN: 978-1-80074-934-4

This is a work of fiction.
Names, characters, places and incidents originate from the writer's
imagination. Any resemblance to actual persons, living or dead, is
purely coincidental.

First Published in 2024

Olympia Publishers
Tallis House
2 Tallis Street
London
EC4Y 0AB

Printed in Great Britain

Acknowledgements

Thank you to the village, people and animals of Appleton Roebuck for inspiring me to write this story.

Contents

A Word From The Author	11
Chapter 1	13
Chapter 2	20
Chapter 3	24
Chapter 4	26
Chapter 5	32
Chapter 6	36
Chapter 7	41
Chapter 8	52
Chapter 9	56
Chapter 10	62
Chapter 11	72
Chapter 12	80
Chapter 13	83
Chapter 14	90
Chapter 15	97
Chapter 16	102
Chapter 17	105
Chapter 18	111
Chapter 19	124
Chapter 20	129
Chapter 21	134
Chapter 22	142
Chapter 23	149
Chapter 24	152
Chapter 25	160

A Word from the Author

Appleton Roebuck is a small, rather ordinary village no more than a handful of miles outside of the ancient city of York in North Yorkshire. There can't be more than two hundred houses with two pubs, a small primary school on the main street and a garage where you can get your car repaired and fill up on fuel… that's it!

It's very quiet and tranquil. The people who live there like it that way.

Just off the main street, down a dusty, heavily potholed track, there hides a house, well… a bungalow really and inside, there lives a man… an unremarkable man, someone you would pass in the street without a second glance.

This story is about him…or to be more accurate… something that happened to him, which changed his world forever.

The story begins…

Chapter 1

'Jack... Jack... Come out of there,' John said in a mixture of a raised voice and a whisper to his Jack Russell terrier who was busy having a good sniff-around in the front garden of the biggest house on the lane. Church Lane wasn't really a lane, more a dirt track with dozens of potholes which had grown to such massive proportions over time, that they were more like craters than potholes.

John's new house was a bungalow which he fell in love with the moment he saw it advertised in the local paper. From the pictures, he could see it was in a rather dilapidated state and would need plenty of TLC. The previous owners, a father and son combo whom John had nicknamed Mister Bodge-it and Mister Scarper, had tried their best to look after it on a shoestring budget but DIY obviously wasn't their thing and, well to be frank, just about everything needed ripping out and starting again.

'Get that horrible little dog off my property,' came a somewhat shrill cry from an open upstairs window to the large house. It was a middle-aged woman waving a rather oversized hair brush at Jack as he calmly trotted about her garden, over the grass and in and out of the flowers of her considerably well-kept borders.

'Jack... sorry... sorry,' shouted John waving apologetically at the irate woman. 'Jack... come here.' The feisty little terrier lifted his head to see what all the fuss was about and slowly squeezed his body through a gap in the hedge to make his way back onto the pot-holed lane… or track, whichever you prefer.

'Yoouu… come on let's get to our new place,' said John as he jogged along the track to his new bungalow with Jack trotting by his side. It was about fifty yards further along on the opposite side where there were no properties… apart from his bungalow. That was one of the main features that attracted John to it so much.

No neighbours… on his side of the lane at least.

There was a large ancient ditch with a trickle of water running through, or stream if you were feeling romantic, which bordered two sides of the property and a rather rickety old bridge that you had to cross to get onto his land and to the bungalow.

The bridge didn't look too bad, although it was obvious it needed some attention. It had been in use for many years and wasn't going to collapse tomorrow, but nevertheless, it would be wise to check it out sooner rather than later.

The amount of water in the ditch could vary from completely dry in high summer to a ten feet deep raging torrent in winter after there had been plenty of heavy rain. John had been assured by Bodge-it and Scarper that the property had never flooded… at least not that they could remember.

The moment John walked over the bridge and through the six-feet-tall wooden double gates he knew he was going to be happy at Beckside. He stopped for a moment on the half-mud, half-gravel driveway leading up to the house, and slowly looked around.

Suddenly a strange feeling swept over him. He couldn't describe it but it was as if he was being watched. He looked down and Jack was between his legs inching backwards slightly and shaking.

'Do you feel it too Jack?'

His loyal companion looked up at him and then back at the house and John could see the look of confusion on his fury little face... should he stay between John's legs or should he run towards the house as his cute little nose busily sniffed aroundfor all the new smells.

'Don't worry. I'm sure it's just that it's new... go on... off you go,' said John waving his hand towards the house. Jack slowly took a step forward... then another... and all of a sudden as if someone had shot a starting pistol into the air he scampered off down the drive towards the house and disappeared round the back.

John still felt as if he was being watched as he walked up to the larger-than-normal front door. He knew Bodge-it and Scarper had vacated the house days before and the place was empty... or was it?

Earlier that day, the lady from the estate agents had given him two keys to the property. It was easy to see which one fitted the front door as one was small, like a key for a Yale lock, which he could see was on the front door, and the other was huge, about five inches long and rusty and obviously fitted an old lock. The small key slid easily into the lock and with a twist and a slight push, the door opened with a creak and a judder. He hesitated for a second before stepping into the large hallway.

'Helloooo,' he called out, with no replyas you would expect from an empty house.

Just as he took another step forward there was a loud thump behind him followed by something sliding along the floor and the sound of paws with claws frantically trying to get traction on the shiny wooden surface.

'Bloody hell Jack,' cried John spinning round, 'you nearly scared me half to death.'

Jack had finished his tour of the grounds and thought it was a good idea to run and jump through the open front door as fast as he could. He was unable to stop and slid past John crashing into the bottom of the staircase which led to the single room upstairs.

The house was officially a bungalow but it had a small dormer room built into the attic space that was classed as an occasional room.

Jack left tiny muddy footprints all over the floor with a long dirty slide mark terminating at the bottom of the stairs. He stood motionless with all four of his legs locked at the knees staring with his big brown eyes directly at John and then, with a thrash of his spinning legs, ran around the house at maximum speed exploring every room.

The battered old removal van with its three burly men came and went, leaving piles of boxes, some half-opened and some not, in each room. Unpacking was easy, the difficult part was deciding where to put everything.

John's previous house had only been small so he didn't have much stuff and once everything was unpacked, the new place still looked half empty… I think the word is… minimalist.

'There… that didn't take long did it Jack,' said John hanging up the last of his clothes in the built-in wardrobe in the room he had decided to make his bedroom. There were three rooms he could have chosen as his bedroom but after selling off his old, well-used, free-standing wardrobe before leaving his last place, the decision was easy.

This room was furthest from the bathroom and the window had the worst of the views but it would do. It looked out onto the driveway which ran the full length of the plot from the bridge and the gates at the front, down the side of the house to the garage in the back, but John wasn't bothered...The built-in wardrobes mattered more. This was to be his room.

Jack had been sitting patiently by the front door for the last half hour which was his way of saying, 'I need to go out,' so John grabbed his lead which was on the table in the large hallway causing Jack to get extremely excited. He loved to jump up and grab the lead and walk off with it, tugging as he went, as if he was taking his human for a walk... not the other way around. Once outside in the dark, they walked around the house and into the field that was on the opposite side of the house to the driveway, where Jack let go of his lead and ran off into the darkness.

John knew about the field from the previous owners and had seen it when he visited before his purchase but didn't realise just how untouched it was. As he walked around it in the dark it was evident that it hadn't been ploughed or used... well... for anything really, for ages. The grass had formed huge mounds like it does when it hasn't been cut for a very long time, and there were bramble bushes everywhere. Some of the brambles were as high as the bungalow... and as wide... and so thick and dense it was impossible to see through them. There were wildflowers and weeds, with some growing as tall as he was. Even in the long shadows created by the moonlight and the lights from the house, it looked beautiful. Just what John wanted and one of the reasons he had bought the place. Seclusion and back-to-nature.

'Come on Jack,' he called, suddenly feeling a little vulnerable standing in the middle of a very dark field he knew nothing about. He could hear Jack puffing and panting as his four little legs pounded their way through the overgrown vegetation and then, for no reason at all, he had that feeling he had earlier.

He felt as if he was being watched.

There was rustling in the bushes away to his left… and then again directly in front of him about 30 yards away and neither of them was Jack because he suddenly appeared out of the blackness by his side. He was soaking wet from the night dew that settles on the vegetation after the sun's gone down and covered in bits of foliage from where he had pushed and wiggled his way through the myriad of bushes in the field.

'About time… Where have you been?' John said glad to see him. 'Come on. Let's get back inside.'

The pair of them made their way back to the house, using the back door instead of the front this time. John wanted Jack to get used to using the back because he knew in the future if Jack was covered in mud, it would be much easier to wipe him down in the sunroom at the rear of the house rather than get mud all over the front hallway.

After a rather late dinner and a well-needed shower for John, the two of them were ready for bed.

'Come on Jack… bedtime.'

Jack followed John to the bedroom and immediately jumped up onto the bed. He had always slept on the bed, I know some people think it's a bad thing to allow a dog on the bed, but Jack was only small, and John was on his own… so who cares. It had been a long day for the pair of them and it didn't take long for them both to fall asleep, with Jack sprawled across the bed as usual leaving only a small section for John.

It was pitch black in the room and suddenly Jack sat bolt upright… growling. John woke bleary-eyed.

'What is it?'

Jack looked at him and then back at the window… he could

hear footprints in the gravel. Lots of footprints. John jumped out of bed followed by Jack who was still growling, and pulled back the corner of the curtains to look onto the driveway. He could still hear the footprints but could see nothing. He moved his head closer to the window to look further along the driveway when a face suddenly appeared at the window startling John so much he nearly jumped out of his skin.

'What the…'

It was followed by another… and another. It was deer. Lots of them. Stags with horns, smaller females and babies… whatever baby deer are called. Fawns I think.

John burst out laughing but Jack couldn't see the funny side of it and was running backwards and forwards from the bedroom to the front door, all the time barking like a dog possessed.

'Jack… Jack… It's fine. It's only deer.'

John picked Jack up and put his nose to the window so he could see what was happening. He growled once or twice as the deer continued to walk past but soon realised they weren't a threat and stopped. John threw Jack back on the bed and climbed in.

It was their first night and if this was anything to go by, they were probably going to have many more like it.

Chapter 2

John and Jack had now lived in their new house for just over a week and it was such a beautiful warm, sunny Sunday morning that it was a good excuse to explore the overgrown field next to the house.

'Come on Jack. Let's go for a walk in the field,' said John as he picked up Jack's lead which was loosely curled up on the small, low and somewhat rickety, homemade table in the sun room at the back of the house. Jack was dozing in his bed at the bottom of the stairs in the hallway, but the moment he heard the word walk, he was up and scooting across the floor towards the back door. As usual, he jumped up as if on springs, taking hold of his end of the lead in his mouth and pulled John out of the door into the back garden.

At one time there had been a flimsy and dilapidated old fence that separated the field from the house but that had collapsed many years ago and mostly crumbled away so it took only a step or two to actually get into the field. Jack immediately let go of his lead and bounced off into the four-foot-high grass, disappearing instantly from view. John couldn't see where he was but could hear him barking and yelping in excitement, so he wasn't worried about losing him… plus he knew Jack never ran away… he might get a little over-enthusiastic at times and forget how far away he was, but he always came back.

John decided to start walking around the perimeter of the field in an anti-clockwise direction… it didn't matter which way he went but seeing as he was at this end which was bordered on its left by the ditch and stream it seemed the logical thing to do.

All around the perimeter of the field on three sides was a very dense area of gorse bushes about ten feet deep, and then trees that must have been many decades old, if not hundreds of years old.

Some of them were huge... especially the Oak trees... of which there were many. This meant it was almost impossible to walk near the edge of the field and the study of the boundary had to be confined to peering into the dense undergrowth through the gorse bushes, which wasn't easy.

One thing that quickly became apparent was the large amount of wildlife.

In every bush and tree, there were birds and squirrels, and in the field sometimes he would catch a glimpse of deer, large and small, a fox and some cubs, and even a couple of badgers which seemed unusual because surely they would be asleep in their underground den during the day.

It was extremely difficult walking through the waist-high grass and stumbling every few feet because of the sheer number of grass sods that had grown to massive proportions over the years. Criss-crossing the uneven ground were thousands of prickly bramble tentacles intertwined with the grass making them almost invisible, which meant it was incredibly easy to get caught up and go flying head-first into the nearest bramble bush.

As John slowly made his way along the edge of the field keeping his eye on Jack who was having a ball of a time running back and forth exploring every new smell, he came across what looked like a wooden shack almost completely hidden by six-foot high nettles and strangling ivy covering every panel, including its roof. He tried for a few minutes to get close enough to have a good look but the fear of getting covered in nettle stings was greater than his curiosity so he gave up and began to circle round. It was only when he got level with its open side that he could see it wasn't a shack at all, it was an old railway carriage. What on earth was that doing in a field? The railway line was at least a mile away… Another conundrum.

Slowly he made his way past the carriage and along the top of the field, which was very much the same as the rest. Once round the top corner, the field bordered a small coppice of mainly ash and beech trees, which extended back to his house where it finished and his land began.

As John approached the land at the rear of his house, he turned his attention to the centre of the field and quickly realised he hadn't seen Jack for a while.

'Jack.' He cried out… Nothing. 'Jack… come on… over here.' He called out again. Still nothing.

All of a sudden he heard a very quiet voice, or to be more precise, he felt a voice.

'He's over there in the centre.'

He spun round on the spot nearly falling over in the process, looking first one in direction and then the other.

'Who said that? Who's there?'

There was no reply. Slowly he walked towards the huge gorse bush in the centre trying not to get his feet caught under the thorny feelers when he caught a glimpse of something white, right in the centre. It moved. It was Jack.

'Come on Jack… out of there… what're you doin'?'

Jack must have heard him that time because John could just see his little head prick up and then wriggle and twist his way through the bush until he was out and clear.

'What have you been doing Jack, you're all wet?'

Jack looked up and began to do the wet-dog-shake that all dog owners will be familiar with, showering John with water and covering him in dirty, muddy spray.

'AAWW JACK... stop it.'

Once jack had finished doing the shake-and-wag, he just stood there looking up at John as if to say, 'Yeh... what do you want?'

'Where did you get wet Jack? There's no water around here. I've just walked all the way round this field and it's completely dry.'

Obviously, there was no answer from Jack... He's a dog.

John turned and peered into the dense growth of the gorse bush. Moving his head from one side to another he could just make out something shimmering right in the centre. He could also see what looked like a tree trunk... or something large, brown and upright. A standing dead body maybe? No. A tree trunk is much more likely.

After standing there for a few minutes contemplating what to do next, Jack was obviously bored and began to whimper.

'OK... OK... I get the idea. Come on then, let's go... we can explore what's in there another day.'

Chapter 3

Midnight had come and gone, meaning the bedroom was pitch black with not a glimmer of light anywhere. This total darkness was something John would have to get used to. He had lived in cities all his life and there was always light from something making its way into the bedroom... but not here in the countryside. If there was no silvery light from the moon, there was no light at all.

He was laid on his back, looking up to the ceiling, with his arm draped over Jack who was laid stretched out next to him. He couldn't get to sleep thinking about the voice he heard earlier in the field.

Who was it? Where were they? Was it someone from down the lane come visiting...? If so why hadn't they shown themselves?

If it was a visitor, he didn't like the idea of them just wandering on to his property so maybe he should keep the large wooden gates shut all the time, which wouldn't be such a bad thing... at least it would be completely private, which, after all, was one of the main reasons he had bought the house in the first place.

He gave a huge, long yawn and slowly began to drift off when, suddenly, in a half-asleep, half-awake state he could hear multiple footsteps in the gravel, outside on the drive. He didn't worry this time and just let himself relax even more because he knew it was only the deer making their nightly walk around the house… but then he could hear, or thought he could hear, maybe he was dreaming, very quiet voices just murmuring along with the footsteps. The voices were so soft with general chitter chatter that they just sent him deeper into a much-needed restful sleep.

The following morning the sun streamed around the curtains and into his bedroom, which along with the constant singing and coo-cooing of birds outside his window, woke him from his sleep. The bird song he could put up with but the rhythmical cooing from the woodpigeons was enough to send a man mad.

He turned onto his back and was just about to cry out STOP THAT BLOODY COOING when he remembered the voices from last night. Were they real or had he been dreaming?

All of John's life he had believed in the paranormal and ghosts.

His mother even thought he might be psychic because of the number of times as a child she would find him sitting in a corner of their terraced house, talking to his imaginary friends. When she casually questioned him about them he would always defend them, saying they were not imaginary and they were his friends. As he got older he grew out of talking to people that weren't there, but he always retained his belief in ghosts and from time to time he would think he could hear something, or see something out of the corner of his eye. Maybe the voice he thought he heard in the field and the voices from last night were just voices from the past… who knows? Anyway… this house was starting to reveal some very strange happenings.

Jack slowly stood up from where he had been sleeping on the bed and had a long stretch with a huge yawn before plonking both his front legs on John's chest and licking his face.

'AAWW… Jack… OK… I know. Time to get up.'

Chapter 4

John had been waiting for a good day to check out the huge gorse bush in the centre of the field… and today was it. It was a beautiful sunny morning with hardly a cloud in the sky and just the smallest breeze wafting by from the south, which meant it was going to be warm.

'Come on Jack, let's go do some exploring in the field.' Well… Jack didn't need to be told twice, he ran and got his lead from the sun room, trotting back with it in his mouth and sitting at John's feet. John opened the back door and Jack shot out, dropping his lead on the patio and disappearing into the field with yelps of excitement.

'Don't get muddy,' cried John after him, knowing fine well that it didn't matter what he said, once Jack was in a field with his nose down, soaking up all the wonderful smells he would run through the muddiest puddle without a care in the world.

The gorse bush in the centre was so huge it took less than a dozen steps or so to reach its outer edge. Over many years the brambles had grown from ground level to a height of about thirty feet.

'I suppose the first thing I should do is walk round this thing and see just how big it is,' said John aloud, even though the nearest person was probably over a hundred yards away in one of the houses further down the track… and Jack certainly wasn't listening.

He decided to go anti-clockwise, for no reason other than he was already pointing in that direction.

Off he set soaking up the warmth from the glorious sunshine and marvelling at the sheer abundance of the different types of wild flowers and plants, most of which he didn't have a clue what they were, although he did recognise the ones we all know. Dandelions, Buttercups, Thistles, Bluebells... Bluebells? Aren't they supposed to grow in wooded areas he thought? That much he did know.

As he wandered round he could see a myriad of wildlife, much more than he had ever seen before. Maybe it was just because he was becoming better attuned to his surroundings... or maybe there was more wildlife here than anywhere else... but that can't be so... why would there be? This place was no different from any other place set in the country.

All of a sudden he heard a voice. Not a loud voice but a calm and unruffled kind of voice. Nothing like the woman from the house down the lane who had shrieked at Jack to get out of her garden.

'Shoo... go on... off with you.'

And then he heard Jack bark.

Was it the same voice he heard before and had the person returned? The commotion was coming from further up the field so John picked up the pace and made his way towards Jack's barking, which wasn't angry barking, more a sort of recognition that someone-was-there kind of bark. As he got closer he could see Jack sitting upright in a small clearing looking at something just out of view behind a holly bush. He was quiet now and obviously happy with whatever or whoever it was because he could see his tail whipping from side to side... always a good sign.

'Good boy.' There it was again... the mellow voice.

'Hello,' called John. 'Good morning. Hello.'

But there was no reply so he ran towards the eight-foot-high holly bush where Jack was sitting, only to find an extremely large Stag deer looking him straight in the face.

John stopped dead in his tracks and toppled backwards into a heap on the grass. The Stag lifted his front hooves off the ground and kicked them both forwards, dropping its head down, brandishing its antlers towards John and then turning and bouncing off into the bushes. John was gobsmacked and lost for words for a few seconds as he got himself to his feet.

'Hello… is there anyone there?' He called looking around, expecting to see a man, a woman, someone, anyone. Surely someone must have been talking to Jack.

But there was no answer, just like earlier.

Now he was starting to get a little annoyed at this person, or persons. Who was it?

Jack ran off into the bushes after the deer so John brushed himself down and continued his trek around the huge, overgrown gorse bush in the centre of the field all the while thinking about who could be in the field.

He soon walked around the gorse bush and was back to the point where he had started, still not knowing any more, apart from the obvious thing that the bush was huge and surrounded by an almost impenetrable wall of prickly gorse… oh, and more wild flowers and plants than he had ever seen before.

After much deliberation, John realised the only way he was going to get into the middle of the huge gorse bush was on his hands and knees and crawl… or be torn to pieces… but where was the best place to start?

Earlier when he had walked around the bush surveying its outer edge, he had seen many indentations and openings that appeared to be entrances, but they were much too small, the vast majority of them were only big enough for small creatures such as mice, rats, rabbits, hares and so on but then he remembered... around the other side, near to where he had seen the stag, there was an opening that he could probably just squeeze himself through.

As quickly as he was able, he made his way round the other side lifting each leg high in the air to avoid tripping over the overgrown clumps of grass, laughing to himself that if anyone could see him they would think he was wearing flippers... and there it was, just where he remembered. The camouflaged opening was about three feet tall and a foot or so wide, almost completely hidden from view by bindweed with its beautiful white flowers and masses of juicy blackberries from the brambles around the edge.

There was no time like the present, so he dropped to his knees and pushed his slim but muscular frame through the entrance and into the dense bush where the amount of light streaming in immediately reduced, making it rather dingy, and a little scary. It was obviously well used because there was not a speck of vegetation on the dry, dusty ground and the sides were completely free of any prickles making it much easier to move than he originally anticipated.

Inching his way along by doing a sideways shuffle one hand and one knee at a time, he could see through the brown prickly gorse, animals of all shapes and sizes, from mice to rabbits, to a badger which turned and disappeared as soon as it saw him. They were doing the same as he was... making their way into the centre through all the well-worn tunnels, which seemed very strange because he hadn't noticed them when he had walked around outside. This particular entrance tunnel didn't go directly to the centre and after a couple of yards, was joined by many smaller tunnels with a multitude of different types of animals... field mice, wood mice, rats, voles... all scurrying about and darting between his hands and knees as he moved along.

'Eeyuk.... I hate rats,' he exclaimed lifting his hands off the ground as a couple scampered by, heading for whatever it was in the centre of the massive bush.

It was getting quite dark in the tunnel with all the gorse bush and undergrowth around him but he could just make out a golden glow shimmering up ahead. He had seen something shimmering the other day when Jack was in here but it wasn't gold in colour, so what was this?

His curiosity overcame his fear of rats and all things small and furry, as he threw himself forward landing head-first in a small clearing. His face was only inches away from a pool of glimmering, golden water at the base of a tree.

Now, he didn't know the names for many trees but he knew this one... it was a Yew tree. He pulled his legs round from behind him and sat cross-legged beneath the tree at the edge of the pool of water.

It was surreal.

He leaned forward and cupping his hand he scooped a handful of the crystal-clear water and after sipping it first, just to make sure it was Ok, gulped it down. It tasted different, sort of sweet. Around the small pond were dozens of animals all taking turns to dip their heads forward and drink the shimmering water. There were as many different types of small animals as you could imagine. Immediately next to him was a ginger cat, who was next to a baby dear and its mother, who was next to two badgers with a large brown rat on the end, who was next to Jack.

'Jack. What are you doing here?' he said amazed to see him

here with all the animals. He raised his head from drinking the water and looked straight at John before sitting back and licking his lips.

All the time John had been sat watching these creatures, he could hear… or better described as feel, quietly spoken voices all around him which until that moment in time he hadn't noticed… or hadn't registered in his mind.

What was going on? Where were these voices coming from? He pushed his hands over his ears to try and block them out but they were still there… in his head.

'STOOOOOOOP,' he cried out. All the animals stopped their drinking and looked up at him.

'Sshh,' he heard in his head as he looked around at them all. Surely the voices weren't coming from the animals… It wasn't possible.

'I've got to get out of here' He yelled, turning around and scrambling along the tunnel towards the light from the sun outside. He scrambled as fast as he could through the bramble tunnel, falling out and onto the grass where he flipped himself over, and in the shadow of the huge bush he lay motionless, staring up into the blue sky.

What had he just witnessed? Animals can't talk.

Chapter 5

Several days had passed since the animal-talking incident in the field and the experience had never left John's mind.

Animals don't talk.

He had tried to convince himself that he must have been dreaming, either that or he was going mad and he had deliberately not ventured into the field again to avoid any of the wildlife. There was no way he wanted to get into a situation where he would put his sanity into question. Jack had been around all the time but John had gone out of his way to avoid him, which made him feel extremely guilty as Jack had always been his best friend, in fact, more like a brother, or a son.

But today was different.

It was a lovely day with the sun beating down and John knew he had to cut the grass today otherwise it would be too long to cut easily if he left it much longer.

As John mowed the grass, Jack was outside with him as usual, sitting on the already-mown section of the lawn just watching the world go by and soaking up the heat from the sun. John was slowly and methodically going up and down the lawn making beautiful contrasting lines as he went, stopping now and again to empty the grass box onto the every-increasing-in-size compost heap at the side of the garage. Every time he stopped mowing Jack had stayed exactly where he was until now, he slowly stood up, gave a long stretch and leisurely trundled off into the field. John stood motionless for a second watching him saunter off knowing exactly where he was going... he was heading for the huge bush in the centre where he seemed to spend more and more of his time, but that was Ok... It was shelter from the heat for him and at least he knew where he was... not getting into trouble chasing the Postman... which he had done often when they first moved in.

It wasn't long before the ritual grass-cutting was completed for another week and a long-deserved drink was had. John sat at the rickety old wooden table and bench inherited from Bodge-It and Scarper, the previous owners and sipped at his cool, refreshing drink of homemade apple juice.

As with just about everything else in the house, the table and bench had been attacked by the DIY-Disaster-Duo and were cobbled together from bits of scrap wood taken from old pallets, fences, garden gates, and even an old kitchen table, and the result was something that had to be treated with care and respect or it would collapse in a heap on the patio.

As John sat gingerly on the creaking, wobbly bench sipping his apple juice, he saw Jack squeeze his way out of the gorse bush, through a hole he hadn't seen him use before... mind you, there were so many entrances and holes in and out of the giant gorse it was easy to miss another one. Jack sauntered his way back along, a now obvious path through the uneven grass and tall wild flowers to where John was sat, where he wandered past towards the door of the sun room.

'A drink... I could do with one of those.'

John spun round in disbelief causing the wooden seat to completely collapse in a cloud of rotten old wood-worm-riddled timber, leaving Jack to continue into the house as he lay in a heap on the patio surrounded by what looked like the beginnings of a bonfire.

'Wha…' he gasped unable to form any kind of a word properly for a second. 'Did you just say something Jack?' Jack didn't reply as he was already in the house having a drink of water from his bowl in the kitchen… and anyway, he probably didn't hear what John said.

'Jack… Jack,' called John scrambling to his feet and crushing bits of rotten wood underfoot as he stumbled through the sunroom door. 'Can you talk now… like the other animals?'

As John stood at the door from the sunroom into the kitchen Jack continued to lap water from his bowl for a few seconds before lifting his head and turning to look at him.

'Well… Can you?'

'I've always been able to talk… and so have the others… YOU and other people just haven't been able to hear us.'

John came over all queasy and began to feel sick so he stepped over to the kitchen sink, ran the tap and threw cold, refreshing water over his face… again and again.

'This cannot be happening.' He mumbled to himself as he leaned forwards and put his head under the running water.

'I'm off to bed,' Jack said wandering towards his bed in the hallway and oblivious to the way John was feeling, after all, as he said earlier… he's always been able to talk.

'No… no… no…' John cried out holding his head in his hands. 'This isn't happening. I must be dreaming.'

'Nope,' said Jack, 'now keep it down will you, I've had a hard day lounging around in the sun and I could do with some shut-eye.'

John threw his arms out to the side and let them drop down slapping against his thighs.

'Oo… err… excuse me…' he exclaimed loudly. 'But wasn't it me who did all the work? I was the one who cut the grass…

what the hell am I doing… I'm arguing with a talking dog… I need to lie down.'

'Do it quietly will you?' said Jack calmly, already starting to nod off.

John ran into the bedroom slamming the door behind him and throwing himself onto the bed.

Jack yawned a huge yawn as dogs do, licked his lips and plonked his head down on his soft bouncy bed.

'Call that quietly.'

Chapter 6

Time flew by at Beckside like it does for all of us.

One minute you're just starting school, then in the blink of an eye, you're leaving to join the big wide world and get a job.

It was no different for John and, in what seemed no time at all, he and Jack had enjoyed many wonderful years at their new house, which of course was no longer new… In fact, the house was and had never been a house… it was a bungalow with a small room upstairs looking out through a dorma window that Bodge-It and Scarper had added so many years before.

They had made a mess of the work as they usually did and it was built so high in the roof that, unless you were a giant, you had to stand on a chair to open any of the windows… which meant that if it was opened during the summer, generally, it wasn't closed again until the winter.

It took a while but John finally succumbed to the fact that Jack and the other animals could talk and even continued to drink the water from under the Yew tree.

He liked it's somewhat unique flavour so much that he ran a pipe from the pond to a hand pump he installed next to the back door on the patio. It had a taste he couldn't describe and made him feel warm inside when he had a mouthful, like having a hot toddy on a cold day without the alcohol and inevitably poorly head when you had too many. The water pump was a traditional old hand pump he had found in one of the fields further up the track and after some bartering with the farmer, they finally agreed he could take it if John repaired his broken gate to the field… which he gladly did.

Having drinking water outside turned out to be a great idea and was taken advantage of, not only by John pumping water to quench his thirst from gardening and general maintenance but by many of the local wildlife, such as squirrels, mice, crows, blackbirds, sparrows and many, many more, so many in fact, John had to build a couple of small ramps and ledges for the animals to use as they came and went. There was a catch-bucket under the pump where all the excess water was stored and soon after installing it, John had rescued a couple of mice calling for help who had fallen in… hence the ramps and ledges.

'Jack,' called John like a father would to one of his children. 'Have you been playing with my socks?'

'Nope,' replied Jack half asleep in his bed. 'But I did see Cyril dragging one across the front lawn earlier.'

Cyril was a mischievous three-legged squirrel that generally kept himself to himself but occasionally would come to the bungalow if he wanted something, and it looks like he needed one of John's socks for some reason.

John slipped his feet into his shoes which he had made from old cut-down wellington boots, and walked slowly out of the front door looking around him as he went. Cyril and his sock were nowhere to be seen until he approached the gigantic horse chestnut trees near the front fence. About seven or eight feet up dangling from a short twig on the trunk of the right-hand tree was his sock… and no sign of Cyril, so after a bit of jumping-on-the-spot, thrown in with some running and jumping he managed to retrieve his sock.

'That bloomin' squirrel,' muttered John to himself as he

made his way back to the house.

Back inside the bungalow he put on his now-found socks and swapped his DIY rubber shoes for his heavy work boots because he had decided that today was the day that the remains of the huge gorse bush were coming down.

Over the years John and the animals had become such good friends, like family almost, and the one most important thing that the majority of them wanted was to get rid of the prickly gorse bush so they could get to the water in the pond easily. The small animals weren't too bothered as they were able to slip in and out without getting caught on the prickles, but the larger ones found it difficult and were always snagging their fur and sometimes causing a small wound, so John agreed to remove the gorse bush… and now after many, many months of slowly removing it bit-by-bit, there was only a small amount left, meaning that today would be the day that it was all finally removed.

It had taken years with some huge bonfires to get rid of the rubbish, which panicked John every time he knew he had to light a fire, because not long ago, after lighting a bonfire he could hear someone or something coughing and spluttering. With the fire popping and crackling he could only just make out the noise, but after a bit of rooting around in the bonfire, trying to take gulps of fresh air away from the clouds of billowing white smoke, he found a rather indignant hedgehog which he managed to pull out and away from the smoke.

'Sorry,' said John to the hedgehog as he carried it over to the edge of the field that joined the woods behind the bungalow. He carefully placed him on the ground and watched him immediately trundle off into the undergrowth without a word. The shock of nearly barbequing one of the animals had disturbed John so he was always reluctant to have a bonfire, but if he did, he spent ages making sure it was completely free of any animals… as best as he could.

It wouldn't take long to clear the remainder of the gorse bush away because he was now well-practised at the best way to remove it… which was to start as close to the centre as he could by chopping through the branches and then pulling the tangled mess away as hard as he was able, piling the offcuts up to form the bonfire on one side in the field.

By early afternoon, the gorse bush was no more, leaving just the Yew tree standing like a prehistoric umbrella over the small golden pond beneath. There was a huge pile of twisted, entangled, dried-out gorse bushes further down the field ready to be burnt. But before anything else… a drink. He walked over to the pump and worked the old handle up and down a few times catching the water in a pewter goblet he had found buried in the field. It was ideal for using outside because it never rusted and was almost indestructible… apart from a few dents and a misshapen handle it was as good as new. The shimmering water slid down his throat warming his insides as it went… not that he needed to warm up, he had built up a nice sweat clearing the bush and now needed something to eat and rest.

This time of year the sun set around seven thirty p.m. so as soon as John had eaten, he made his way back out to the field, torch in hand, and began to walk around making sure there were no animals close by that would be scared by the flames and, using a long piece of wood he began to lift parts of the piled-high offcuts looking for animals and calling as he went.

'Hello… is anyone in there… Hello… Hello.' He was just about to give it the all-clear when he heard a snuffling sound and then a sneeze, so pushing his long piece of wood deep into the unlit bonfire he called out again.

'Hello…'

'Pff… ppff… atishoo… atishoo.'

John pointed his brightly-lit torch into the gloom of the soon-to-be-lit bonfire only to see the hedgehog again... the same one he rescued before.

'Come on you... out.' He bent down to pick him up but the grumpy hedgehog refused.

'I don't need you to help.' He snuffled. 'Leave me be. I'm off back into the woods... it's much safer in there... not as warm but certainly safer.'

Once the hedgehog was well clear, John began to light the fire using the long stick he had used earlier, with the end wrapped in an oil-soaked cloth. It burnt well and was long enough to push deep inside the bonfire. It was almost completely dark by now and with the cut-off branches being extremely dry, the fire reached about twenty feet tall in no time.

As with any bonfire John had learnt it was good practice to watch and stay with the fire until it had reduced to a size where it couldn't cause any damage, such as embers flying off, landing on the bungalow roof and nearly burning it to the ground, so he sat on his favourite wooden bench with Jack by his side and soaked up its glowing orange and yellow warmth... snaps and crackles and all.

As the fire slowly got smaller, he could make out faces of animals in the field with their eyes shining amber-yellow from the glowing embers, and if he listened very hard he could hear them talking and chatting, not about anything in particular but just about life and how content and safe they felt at Beckside. John felt the same.

'What more could I want Jack, this is fantastic,' he said stroking Jack who was curled up on his lap. 'What more could I want?'

Chapter 7

Looking back many years, John had only been able to buy Beckside because of the money he inherited by selling his parent's property after they passed away, and so as time passed and John's savings began to dwindle, he and Jack became more and more self-sufficient until there came a point where John couldn't remember the last time he needed, or even wanted, to pass beyond the gates to his property. Over the years he had found or made everything he required to make living in the countryside at Beckside, as easy as he could.

The first thing he had managed to go self-sufficient with, was the food. He turned completely vegetarian, or vegan, obviously. With his ability to communicate with, and befriend all the local animals, there was no way he could do anything else… so now vegetables and fruit were grown in every conceivable place, including the sunroom at the back of the bungalow where it was warm enough all year round to grow grapes. The vines climbed up the walls and along the rafters of the glass roof giving the room a very continental feel.

Vegetables and fruit were stored everywhere in the bungalow and the garage, and every autumn, jams and pickles were made to last the winter and into the next spring.

John had been a mechanical engineer in what seemed another-life-ago, so his engineering background had really helped when it came to finding ways of creating and storing electricity. He had made two quite large water wheels from the rear axle of an old car he had found half buried in one of the fields close by, which after wiring them up to a couple of car alternators and mounting it to the bridge out front, could generate electricity nearly all year round from the water flowing in the stream below. It would occasionally run dry in summer for a short period so he also made two wind turbines, again from a couple of car alternators, which helped to charge the batteries when the stream didn't flow. He had managed to accumulate a large store of old car batteries over the years and the only thing he had to buy was a rather hefty DC-AC inverter to power his fridge, kettle and lighting. He had done away with his TV, radio and phone many years ago, realising that he had everything he had ever wanted at Beckside, so why bother with the outside world? He had plenty of his animal friends to talk to and keep him company if he felt lonely, which to be honest, he never did.

Since he had cleared the gorse bush away from the Yew tree and the pond, the wildlife had flourished. The word must have got round that it was much easier to get to the water, so animals large and small came from miles around to drink from the pond, although it wasn't easy for them at first being so close to a human, but they soon got used to it. For most of them humans only meant one thing… trouble, but the more often they came, the more they got to know John and Jack, and after they had been a few times they just thought of John as another one of them… in fact, John and Jack became so respected by all the animals that many of them would bring their offspring to meet them, and even leave them with John while they rested in the field under the shadow of the great Yew tree.

***

'OW.' Cried Jack standing up and moving a couple of feet to his left where he plonked himself down again in the sun and flopped onto his side.

'Haha... have they nipped your tail again?' Asked John laughing as he pumped some water into his hand and lifted it to his mouth.

'Yes... baby foxes... they're all the same... too inquisitive for their own good.'

'Aww... leave them alone, they're only playing. You're getting too grumpy in your old age.'

John put his head under the spout and pumped the refreshing golden water over his head to cool himself. It was another gloriously hot sunny day and all the animals were doing their best to keep cool, which is why Jack was babysitting the fox cubs. Their mother was drinking some of the honey-coloured pond water and getting a much-needed break from her hyper-active offspring.

After a few minutes or so the mother fox returned for her cubs.

'Thank you for watching my children,' she said bowing her head to John, who bowed his head in return.

'Think nothing of it. It was a pleasure... wasn't it Jack.'

'Oh... Er... Yes,' said Jack somewhat surprised at the question from John as he twisted his body and jumped to his feet.

'It is the first time we have ventured here,' the mother fox said quietly as she sat down. 'Would you mind if I told others, and could we come again?'

John walked slowly over to where she was sitting and knelt on one knee in front of her.

'Of course I don't mind you coming again and you can tell as many others as you like.'

'Thank you,' she replied. 'Come children, we must be off.'

'Before you go, what's your name?' Asked John as he stood up. 'I try and get to know all the animals' names who visit here.'

'Foa... my name is Foa.'

'Nice to meet you Foa. I hope to see you and your children again soon.'

'You will John,' she said turning her head back as she walked away with her cubs.

She couldn't have got more than a few feet before John called out sounding a little confused.

'Foa... wait... how do you know my name?'

She stopped in her tracks and turned to face him.

'Every animal around here knows your name John,' and without a second word, she turned and walked off into the field with her cubs bounding off ahead.

John looked down at Jack who had gone back to laying on the grass.

'You see... I'm famous,' he said with a huge smile creeping across his face.

'Yeah, right,' said Jack turning over onto his back and squirming around with his feet in the air as if he had a huge itch on his back that desperately needed scratching.

Later that afternoon John was weeding the ground between the carrots and runner beans when he heard a voice coming from somewhere. He knew straight away it was an animal of some sort because he didn't hear them speaking in a conventional sense as he would normally through his ears. No, he seemed to feel the voice from animals... deep inside his head. He stood upright and leant on his hoe to look around but couldn't see any animal that might be talking to him, so as anyone would, he went back to his work. Almost immediately he heard the voice again, only this time it was more forceful, still polite, but definitely more forceful. Again he stopped and looked around, but still, he couldn't see who might be calling him.

'Excuse me... down here,' came the voice. He looked down and there in between the rows of carrots he'd just been weeding were three mice.

'I'm sorry,' he said as he knelt to get closer to them. 'I didn't see you down there.'

'John can you help me please,' pleaded the largest of the three mice standing on its hind legs.

'I'll do my best,' smiled John. 'What seems to be the problem?'

'My husband has had a dreadful accident and his back legs don't work. Can you please help? I don't know what I'd do without him. I love him so very much... and our children...' She began to cry pointing at the small mice to her side.

'Oh my. Where is your husband?'

'He is over here,' she said pointing and gesturing for John to follow her over to the cabbages. 'We left him here in the shade of the cabbage leaves.' She beckoned for John to come close so she could whisper. 'Also he is out of sight of cats.'

'I see... let me have a look,' said John trying to sound as if he knew what he was doing as he moved the cabbage leaves to one side. The mice ran towards some recently cut dock leaves and there, laid on the bottom leaf was a mouse.

'We didn't know what to do,' began the female mouse. 'So we laid him on this large leaf and dragged him across the field to come and see you John. All the animals talk about this place ... and you, so I thought... maybe you could help?'

'But I'm not a doctor or a vet... I don't know what to do.'

Then, all of a sudden as he was moving the dock leaves to

check the injured mouse, the two smaller mice, who were obviously their children, jumped onto his hand.

'Please… please… please… please do something to help our dad.'

John was so overwhelmed he didn't know what to say… so he gently put the small mice back on the ground and very carefully put the dock leaf with the mouse into the palm of his hand and stood up.

He could see the mouse was in a lot of distress and pain as it lay on its back unable to move the lower half of its body.

'So… what happened…? Oh… what's your name first?'

'Fus.' He replied with difficulty.

'Ok, Fus… what happened. How did you hurt yourself?'

Fus tried to lift himself onto his elbows to talk but the pain was too much and fell back clenching his sharp little teeth together.

'Our nest is over the other side of the field… by the old wooden bridge into the far field.'

'Yes… I know it,' said John nodding.

'And we were all leaving to go forage for food when a large branch fell from the trees by the stream and hit me… luckily I saw it in time and pushed the children and my wife out the way… but it has damaged my back and I can't feel my legs.'

As soon as Fus mentioned he couldn't feel is legs, John knew it was bad news.

'Do you mind if I move you over onto your front Fus, I want to take a look at where the branch hit your back?'

'No… you do what you have to,' replied Fus trying to roll over, obviously in a great deal of pain.

'Fus… careful… here let me help you,' John said calmly, using the side of his hand to gently push the injured mouse onto his front. 'There... are you OK like that?'

'Yes... I'm fine... how does it look?'

There was a small black mark on Fus' back where the branch must have made contact and as John ran his hand down his spine he could feel it was broken and there was a small gap between the vertebrae... now, John wasn't a vet but he didn't have to be one to realise there was nothing he could do... I mean... you can't mend a broken back, can you?

'How does it look?' Asked Fus nervously.

'Well... I can see where the branch hit you... it hasn't broken the skin.'

'Come on John,' Fus called out unable to turn round and look John in the eye. 'I can't move or feel my legs.'

'John,' said Fus' wife quietly as she walked towards them. 'Can you do anything?'

John felt awful as he put Fus gently back on the ground and watched his wife take hold of her husband's little paw with hers, and the children scampered over and sat next to their mum.

'Look, guys... I'm not a vet... I don't have any medical knowledge at all... but I can see your back is broken Fus... there's nothing I can do.'

Fus' wife began to sob and the children, too young to fully understand what was going on, responded to their mother crying by doing the same and climbing up onto the leaf to be next to their dad.

'John... John...' John heard his name being called quietly and looked around for who was wanting him.

It was Jack who was only a few feet away and had watched and listened to the whole thing.

'John I have an idea.'

'Excuse me,' he said apologetically to the mice. 'What

Jack?' he said turning away and speaking quietly enough that the mouse family couldn't hear him. 'I can't mend bones... or broken backs.'

'I know but...'

'But what Jack?'

'I have heard rumours over the years we have been here, about the healing power of the water in the pond.'

'What... Water can't mend a broken back,' he whispered bending down to get closer to Jack to make sure the mice couldn't hear them.

'I know John... but look at them... without Fus how will the family survive?'

They both turned and watched as all the mice were huddled together on the leaf sobbing and talking to each other... as any normal family would in this situation.

'Ok... You win Jack... I'll give it a try... Fus, I've got an idea and I'd like to try something... that is if you'll let me.'

'Oh... please,' said the wife surprised at John's change of heart. 'Please... anything.'

'Ok... now I don't know if it will work but I'd like to try.' So he got down on one knee and began to scoop Fus up from the leaf into the palms of his hands.

'Excuse me Mrs Fus... children... I just need to take your dad away for a little walk... Jack would you look after these mice for me... I won't be long.'

'Where is he taking him?' They all asked Jack.

'He won't be long,' replied Jack laying down on his belly next to them and doing his best to distract them for a while. 'Now tell me... where do you live and have you lived there long? Do you like it?'

John walked carefully into the middle of the field and to

where the Yew tree was spreading out like a huge umbrella over the small pond beneath. Because it was such a lovely day, there were many animals, large and small, all taking a drink but when they saw John approaching, they all pulled back from its edge and gave him space to get to the water.

He knelt in the shade of the Yew tree and slowly and carefully rolled Fus from the leaf onto his belly into the palm of his left hand while scooping up some of the water with his other and offering it to Fus to drink.

'Here Fus... drink some of this water.'

Fus lapped it up.

'Now what?' said Fus trying to turn round and see what he was doing.

'Hang on.' John replied filling his other palm with water and pouring it over Fus' back.

'Whoa... that's cold.' He cried out as John did it again.

'Are you giving me a bath?'

'No... wait and see.'

But nothing happened.

John poured some of the water over Fus one more time, but again nothing happened.

'I'm sorry Fus... I... I thought it might work'

'Hey... at least you tried.'

John's hands were muddy with leaning on the ground by the pond, so before they returned to the others he wanted to give them a quick wash.

'Fus. I'm just going to lay you here by the pond so I can wash my hands... Ok?'

'Yes Ok.'

'Good.' So John lay the still-injured mouse on the grass and plunged both of his muddy hands into the pond's cold water. As he did so, he felt he wanted to do something he had never done before... Pray... Now John didn't believe in God... or gods... but he did believe in trying to help... so what did he have to lose?

I don't know why this water is here, or who or what placed it here, but if you can hear me... whoever or whatever you are, please help me to help this poor mouse and his family.

Nothing happened but as he continued to wash his hands the water began to shine with a dazzling golden light. It shone so brightly that all the animals around became scared and moved away, hiding behind bushes and clumps of grass, but none were so frightened as to leave, because they knew something wondrous was happening... and being nosey animals, they didn't want to miss a thing.

Without thinking John scooped up some of the honey-coloured water and poured it over Fus, who was so amazed by what he could see that he didn't say a word. Almost immediately the water began to fizz and bubble where it had touched his little furry body.

Once the foaming and fizzing stopped, the water in the pond returned to its natural colour, which by the way was always a slightly golden colour anyway, and John looked at Fus with a huge smile on his face.

'Well, Fus... how do you feel?'

Fus was on his back and without a thought he shook all four of his little limbs and flipped over onto his front where he stood up on his hind legs.

'WOW,' he cried out.

'WOW,' replied John as Fus jumped into the air and did a little back flip.

'Let's go back to the others... don't carry me John, I want to run.'

So they both made their way back to the edge of the field where Fus' family and Jack were waiting patiently, but John made it back first, obviously because he was so much larger with longer legs.

'Oh no,' cried out Fus' wife. 'What's happened to my husband?'

And before John could say anything, Fus darted out from the long grass and ran headlong into his wife knocking her about six inches into the air, which by the way, for a mouse, is very high.

'Fus... Fus... you're Ok.'

'Yep... good as new... maybe even better... who knows?'

His children were so happy they began doing back flips on the grass, something they had learned from their dad, and his wife couldn't stop playing with his ears... that must be a mouse thing?

'Jack... Jack... come on let's leave them alone and go inside for something to eat... I'm starving.'

'Me too... do you know how difficult it is to keep three mice entertained for as long as I did?'

'What about me... I've just performed a miracle?'

'A miracle... phewey... you want to try looking after a family of mice.'

'Let's get something to eat,' said John with a smile.

'Good idea... can I have a tin of dog food... none of that dried stuff today please.'

'Ok... Ok,' said John patting Jack on his back.

Chapter 8

Time passed by, sometimes slowly, sometimes quickly, and every so often the memory of what happened with Fus under the Yew tree would bounce around inside John's head putting a huge smile on his face, which must have looked very strange... witnessing a grown man smiling all of sudden for no reason. But it didn't matter because he never had any visitors anyway... unless you could call the postman putting junk mail in the old tin mailbox attached to the large wooden gates on the bridge, a visitor. He would call, 'Hello... Post,' and then walk back to his van parked on the track. John would call back, 'Thank you,' if he was in the garden somewhere, which he usually was.

Apart from that *Thank you* to the postman and the occasional *Hello* to people out for a walk with their dog who he would see when he opened the gates to collect the mail from the mailbox, John never spoke to another human being. All the conversations he now had were with animals, which he would be the first to admit, initially were a bit limited.

You see, we forget when we talk to someone else, that however much we might think we have nothing in common with the person we're talking to, there is one huge thing that binds us together which allows us to chat about pretty much anything really... we're human... the same species.

For instance. We can always chat about the weather, what we saw on TV last night, or the new car the guy down the road has just bought...

Now… when John is chatting with his animals the only things they have in common is they all live close to each other, sometimes they might be mammals like humans are, but equally they could be birds, spiders, insects, frogs, and pretty much any species you might find in and around the village of Appleton Roebuck, near York, and… over the years John has found that if the animal, insect, spider, or whatever creature, has drunk water from under the Yew tree, then he could talk to it.

*

It was early morning and, as usual, John opened the front door to let some fresh air in while he was standing in the doorway looking out at the two huge horse chestnut trees and shading his eyes from the sunlight, he happened to look down at his feet. There, on the front step was a pile of grain and seeds about the size of his fist.

'Jack,' he called without turning round. 'Have you seen this? Someone or something has left a pile of seeds by the front door.'

Jack gave a yawn, slowly climbed out of his bed at the foot of the stairs and sauntered over to have a look.

'Oh… yes… seeds,' he said sounding very unruffled.

'What I meant was… I wonder why they're there. I wonder who left them?'

'Probably the squirrel… you know what he's like… probably forgot where he left them… he'll be back for them,' said Jack yawning again and hopping over the doorstep to go outside and do what dogs do first thing in the morning.

'You could be right, I'll leave them there in case he comes back for them.'

Later that morning, John was out in the back garden tending to the vegetable patch when he came across a stack of dandelion leaves piled amongst the vegetables and then after an hour or so, some more next to the patio… then a bit further along some more plants that looked like weeds piled up in three separate mounds.

'What the…?' He exclaimed scratching his head and looking round wondering if whoever had done this was still close-by but there wasn't an animal to be seen so he continued hoeing the soil and concentrating on what he was doing.

'Hahem… excuse me,' came a voice from behind him. He stood up, and as he straightened his creaky back he heard the voice again.

'Excuse me… are you John?'

He turned round to see a family of Roe deer standing no more than a few feet away.

'Yes… Yes… I'm John.'

'Good… we wanted to thank you for helping Fus. He and his family are well known around here and as other animals have brought you items to say thank you, we wanted to say thank you in person.'

'Err… thank you… you're welcome,' replied John somewhat surprised that the animals were thanking him for helping the mice.

'There are not many humans who will help us… let alone a small mouse. We have heard you are special. Thank you,' said the largest of the deer who walked towards him and bowed his head, followed by the other deer doing the same, one by one.

'I don't know what to say,' said John still a little dazed that they felt they had to say thank you for something that happened a while ago now, but the deer said no more and turned and slowly walked off into the field where they were soon out of sight hidden by the bushes.

The seeds and the piles of leaves made sense now… it was the animals offering a thank you in ways that only they knew how to. It made John feel quite emotional because it's all right for a human to say thank you… with words, but when an animal offers you food that it has gathered, it means a lot to them… they need that food to survive.

John spent the rest of the day tending to the vegetables and every so often had to break off to talk to the many creatures that came to say thank you.

It was just one of the so many incredible days that made living at Beckside such a wonderful experience and one that he would remember for a very long time.

Chapter 9

Time is a strange thing. When we look back at our lives it feels like one minute we're just going to school, then we leave and get a job. Some people start a family, others become explorers or farmers, or doctors. The next minute we're middle aged wondering where all the time has gone and preparing for the last chapter of our life…but for some, one person to be exact, things can work out very differently…

'Hello… Hello…' came a voice from beyond the gates leading to the outside world. 'Is there anyone there?'

Two men dressed in suits and wearing high-vis waistcoats stood on the bridge over the stream and knocked quite hard on the high, solid wooden gates that marked the entrance to Beckside. A middle-aged woman who regularly walked her dog along the potholed track to the next village was walking past and commented on their attempt at getting the home owners attention.

'I've lived in this village for over thirty years now and I think I've only seen the chap who lives there a handful of times. He's very much a recluse.'

'Does he still live here?' Asked the older of the two men.

'Yes… as far as I know, although no-one has seen him for a long time.'

'How long?'

'Oh… I don't know… many years.'

'How do you know he still lives here… or if he's even still alive?'

'I walk along here regularly, with my dog, and I can often just make out a male figure with a small brown and white terrier, either working at the back of the house, which you can just see through the trees further along, or walking amongst the bushes and around that big tree in the centre of the field,' she said gesturing with her hand towards the field on the left.

The house and field were difficult to see from the track because of the high wooden fence that bordered the stream at the front and the dense, overgrown trees further along and around the edge of the field. The only way you could see into the field or the back of the house was to walk about fifty yards further along the track and peer through a small hole in the trees and bushes that bordered the stream… and even then you couldn't see much.

'How do you know it's the owner, and not a gardener or someone doing some maintenance to the house?' Asked the other man.

'I know it's him… the owner… I haven't seen him often, as I said, but I do recognise him and his little dog… mind you, now I come to think about it, he must have had that dog for over thirty years so it can't be the same dog… it must be another one… I mean… dogs don't live that long do they.'

'No… they don't… Ok… so I'll just have to keep knocking then. Thank you… Mrs…?'

'Ms Walker… Good luck,' she said as she gave them a wave and set off along the track with her beautiful golden retriever who had waited patiently by her side. 'Come on Sky… let's go.'

The older of the two men who was obviously in charge began knocking on the gates again, although this time a lot harder.

'Hello… Hello.'

'What if we walk further along the track and see if we can

see any signs of life?' Suggested the second man.

'Ok… yes… good idea… come on then. The track is dry thank goodness… no mud.'

'Yes. I haven't brought my wellies.'

The two men wandered slowly along the stream bank which was level with the height of the field and the land to the property opposite, with a gap of about twelve to fifteen feet, way too far to jump and about ten feet or so deep, again far too difficult to clamber down and up the other side.

'This place is a real fortress,' joked the younger of the two men.

'Yes… but believe me, there's always a way into these types of places… always.'

It wasn't long before they found the gap in the trees and bushes, and sure enough, they could see a male figure with his dog sitting by his side, standing at the edge of the property looking into the field.

'Hello… Sir.' They both shouted in unison, waving their arms like two oversize human canaries dressed in their bright yellow high-vis waistcoats.

'Hello… Helloooo….' The last hello must have been loud enough because John heard them and gestured for them to go back to the gates on the bridge where they had been knocking a moment earlier.

'Good day gentlemen,' said John politely as he slowly opened one side of the gates which creaked so loudly with rusty hinges that it made the hairs stand up on the back of the two men's necks. 'What can I do for you?'

'Are you the owner of this property sir?' said the older man looking down at some paperwork he was clutching in his hand.

'Yes… that I am.'

'Do you mind confirming your name for me please, as the records we have are rather old and possibly out of date?'

'How old are your records?' Asked John looking down at Jack who had joined them and sat down next to him.

'Well... let me see. It is the land registry details we have and... well, if you tell me your name, I can tell you if they relate to you.'

'My name is John Ryder.'

'Yes... yes. But... but...' The older of the two men stuttered looking a little bewildered.

"Is there a problem?' Asked John now feeling a little confused about this whole thing.

'Have your family lived here as well, Mr Ryder, only...'

'No... just myself, and my dog Jack,' he replied bending over slightly and patting Jack on his back as he sat calmly by his side. 'Only... what, gentlemen?'

'Well, I'm afraid our records must be incorrect.'

'Do you mind if I see that document?' Asked John mystified as to why the document would be wrong. He ran his finger along the lines of text and confirmed to them that the purchase date was correct so what was the problem?

'What is the problem? Mr Ryder... the problem is... that the date shows it was nearly sixty years ago.'

'Sixty years ago... it can't be... that would make me one hundred years old and Jack would be over sixty... It must be wrong,' said John with the smallest sign of a smirk on his face.

'Yes... yes... it must be wrong... I don't know what's gone wrong... I'm sorry Mr Ryder. Anyway, look... we can sort the dates out later but we are here to tell you that the field next to your property has been sold and the new owners want to gain access across your land. They want to begin building as soon as possible.'

'Access... building... build what?' Replied John feeling the colour draining from his cheeks as he spoke and as if he was about to be sick.

'Our clients want to build fifty-seven houses on the field. They have already gained planning permission and now would like to pay you handsomely for a small access road to be built along the front of your property.'

'I... I can't do that. What about the Yew tree, the pond... all the animals?' said John with a definite sense of panic in his voice.

'Don't worry about all that Mr Ryder. Our clients will plant many new trees and relocate any of the endangered species that may be present before work begins.'

John was in so much shock he was unable to speak. His mouth felt dry, he began to sweat, his legs started to shake.

'No... No... Sorry. No...' He pulled the heavy wooden gate towards him and slammed it shut almost catching the younger of the two men's fingers as it closed. He wiggled the rusty locking bolt right the way across making sure it was firmly in place before he walked slowly back to the rear of the house and plonked himself down on his favourite wooden seat. He sat there for ages, completely silent, staring into the field. Jack had heard everything and jumped carefully up onto his lap not knowing what to say.

The two men had achieved what they had come to do... pass on the information. They would then report back so their clients could begin proceedings to gain access to the field... one way or another.

They had a few minutes' walk back to their car because they had parked it on the main road a few hundred yards from Beckside, learning over the years that it was best to leave the car far away from disgruntled victims.

'That lady we talked to on the track said she had lived here for over thirty years and known Mr Ryder all that time... and his little dog... what was it called... Jack? That's weird don't you think?'

'Yes... I don't know what's going on there but something is very peculiar... But anyway, let's get back and file our report... it's up to our clients now.'

'Jack... what are we going to do? They want to flatten the field and build houses.'

'I know John... is there anything we can do?'

'I don't know... I really don't know.'

Chapter 10

The men filed the report to their clients, including the anomaly with the dates on the land registry form, and that was that…

***

'Have you seen this?' asked Denise who was an admin clerk at the company that was going to build on the field next to Beckside. She had worked for the company for eight years and was held in quite high regard as a valuable member of their team.

'Have I seen what?' replied Steve Dickinson without even looking up from his paperwork. He was the head of New Developments and known to be ruthless… if required. He hadn't risen to be the Head of New Developments for nothing.

'This,' said Denise who was standing at his desk, waving around an A4-sized brown folder trying to get his attention and finally thrusting it under his nose.

He opened the folder and thumbed the papers inside, only glancing at the occasional word as he flicked through them and handed them back to her.

'Again I say… What, Denise?'

She tutted and leaning forward, flicked the pages over until she found what she wanted and prodded at a specific place on the page.

'Look… look at his date of birth… and there…' she said turning a few pages over and prodding at some more figures.

'The date he bought Beckside.'

'Well... that would make him about a hundred Denise... it has to be wrong... the figures are wrong.'

'Yes, I know that... the problem is... if the figures are wrong, we are going to have a problem legally trying to buy access across his land. The figures have to be correct.'

'Ok... so what do you suggest?'

'Well... I'm going to York this weekend, why don't I call in to see him and try and get to the bottom of it?'

'Err... Ok... if you think it will help?'

'No harm in trying Steve,' she said with a smile on her face as she turned and walked out of his office waving around the brown folder about Beckside.

***

'Helloooo... Is there anyone there?' said Denise in a slightly raised voice, trying not to sound confrontational in any way. 'Hello...' She peered through the cracks of the gates to Beckside and could see the figure of a man standing at the front door to the bungalow with a small white and brown dog at his feet. 'Excuse me... Mr Ryder.' She called out a bit louder than before. She moved her head from side to side to try and get the best view she could through the multitude of small cracks in the gates and could see him walking towards her and then stopping within a couple of yards from her.

'Mr Ryder?'

'Yes... what do you want?' said John guardedly. Since the unexpected and highly upsetting visit from the two men a few days ago, John was extremely wary of anyone wanting to see him.

'I would like to talk to you if I may.'

'What about?'

'It's rather personal... do you think I could come in instead of shouting it out so everyone could hear.' She pleaded with her nose pressed up against the lichen-covered gates.

John stood motionless for a second just taking a moment to think.

'What do you think, Jack?' he said looking down to where Jack was sitting by his feet.

'What harm can she do... let her in,' said Jack.

John took a couple of steps towards the gates, wiggled back the rusty bolt and opened one side. He was pleasantly surprised by what he saw. Denise was an attractive woman, about five feet seven, slim build, shoulder-length blonde hair and a smile to take your breath away.

'What's your name?'

'Denise... Denise Williamson,' she replied softly. 'Can I come in?'

He gestured with his hand for her to enter and then closed the gate behind her, pushing the bolt across to lock it. Denise suddenly felt very vulnerable... and very stupid... she didn't know this man from Adam, and for all she knew, he was a mass murderer that buried all his victims in his vegetable patch.

'Err... do you have to lock the gates?' She asked nervously.

'Sorry... force of habit,' said John but still leaving the gates locked.

'Are we alone? Only I heard you talking to someone earlier.'

'Oh... that... I was just talking to my dog... Jack,' he said bending down to give him a stroke with both hands. Then he looked her straight in the eye and stood up. 'Now... what do you want to talk to me about?'

'I work for the company that has bought the field next to your house and…'

'Let me stop you there Denise, if I'd known you were from that company I wouldn't have let you in… now… please leave,' he said turning his back on her and taking a step towards the gates.

'No… wait… Mr Ryder. I want to talk to you about the dates on the Land Registry forms… and when you bought the house… Please.'

John stopped in his tracks and stood facing the gate for a second or two before turning to face her.

In the back of his mind, he always knew this moment would come… you can't keep a secret like this forever.

Looking directly at her, he sighed the deepest of sighs.

'Would you like a cup of tea Denise…? Although before you say yes, I warn you… I am completely self-sufficient here so it's nettle tea?'

'Err… yes… thank you… I'll give it a try,' she replied somewhat surprised at his sudden change of heart. One minute he wants to throw her out… the next, he's offering tea.

'Follow me,' he said walking off down the side of the house, gravel crunching underfoot and Jack running off head.

The day was overcast but warm so John asked Denise to take a seat at the wooden bench on the patio while he made some nettle tea.

'Jack… look after Denise while I'm gone… don't get up to any mischief,' he said walking through the door into the sun room and then the kitchen. Denise bent down and took hold of Jack's head in her hands giving him a good rub with her hands.

'He talks to you like you're human doesn't he?'

Jack barked as if answering and Denise stood up to have a good nosey around. The first thing that struck her was the huge number of vegetables being grown at the back of the house, and the second was the openness and sheer beauty of the field next to the house.

'Sorry about that, took a bit longer than I thought,' said John as he placed two mugs of steaming green nettle tea on the small DIY coffee table made of a large up-turned flower pot and a Yorkshire stone flagstone.

'I was just admiring your vegetable patch,' Denise said sitting down and crossing her legs. She was glad we wore her navy-blue trouser suit.

'Yes... many years of hard work.'

The two of them sipped at their tea and it all went silent for a few seconds until Denise spoke.

'So Mr Ryder, the dates... on the documents.'

John stood motionless with his back to Denise, looking out into the field wondering where to start. He turned to face her.

'Denise... do you believe in god, or a higher power?'

'Err... I believe there might be something... up there.' She pointed to the sky. 'But... like everyone, I suppose... I'm not sure... why... what has all that got to do with the dates on the documents?'

'All my life I have never been a believer... about any of it. I just thought that when we died... that was it... I suppose I still do... but living here and seeing what I've seen... well, my views and beliefs have changed somewhat.'

'Mr Ryder... you're losing me?'

'Sorry Denise... by the way call me John... I've never liked being called Mr Ryder.'

'Ok... John... look, I'm completely confused. What has God got to do with my paperwork?'

'Denise... the dates on the forms are correct. I was born on 30 July 1915.'

Denise just stared at him with her mouth slightly open for a couple of seconds.

'I'm sorry John but that just can't be true... why, you would be..."

"One hundred and six years old. Yes. And Jack is seventy one."

She stood up, turned away to face the vegetable patch and burst out laughing, throwing her arms into the air.

'Come on, Mr Ryder... that's just not possible... You maybe could... possibly reach one hundred and six, but you only actually look about forty five, fifty... but no way could Jack be seventy one... no way. What you say is ridiculous."

John sat down on the bench and Jack came to join him sitting between his legs.

'Look. I know it's hard to believe but it's true,' said John taking a sip of his nettle tea and patting Jack with his other hand as if this sort of thing happened all the time.

'Look, John. Stop messing around. This is important.'

'That's not all Denise. I can talk to the animals... and they can talk to me.'

'John. You're scaring me. You sound... crazy. Mad. Mental.' Said Denise sounding slightly panicky and beginning to wish she had never come.

'So you're telling me that not only are you one hundred and six years old, your dog is seventy one years old, and you have conversations with the animals... Do you know how crazy that sounds? If that's so... show me... talk to Jack.'

'Ok… Jack, what do you think of Denise?' Said John looking Jack directly in the eye, but he had forgotten one thing. Although he used his voice to talk to the animals, they spoke to him using their mind, not their voice, so when Jack replied she was unable to see or hear anything happening.

This is all because John and Jack have been shut away for years in their bungalow with hardly any intervention from other human beings. Apart from the postman of course.

'I think she's upset with you John,' replied Jack.

'I think you're right,' said John in answer, although it looked to Denise as if it was just a one-way conversation.

'Mr Ryder. I can't take any more of this nonsense so I'm afraid I'm going to leave now. You need help. You've lived on your own for far too long.'

John stood up as Denise almost leapt out of the chair and walked quickly off down the side of the house towards the gates, crunching through the gravel as she went.

'Hang on Denise I'll open the gates for you.'

She reached the gates well before he did and stood there with her arms crossed desperate to get away from this lunatic and his mad dog.

John took hold of the sliding bolt and jiggled it up and down to move it back enough for the gate to open.

'I really need to oil this,' he said with a half-smile on his face as she pushed past him and out onto the bridge.

'Thank you for the nettle tea Mr Ryder,' she said without turning round.

'What about the dates on the documents?' Called John after her. She stopped on the bridge to his property and turned to face him.

'I think the dates are immaterial now, don't you? You need

medical help and that opens other avenues for the company. I'm sorry Mr Ryder. Good bye,' said Denise swivelling round on the spot and walking briskly off down the lane towards her car.

'I think what she's trying to say is you're mad in the head John,' said Jack who was sat next to the nearest of the large horse chestnut trees.

'I think that went quite well… don't you?' Said John with a smile on his face as he closed and locked the gates.

***

'The man's completely mad. I mean completely, Steve,' said Denise almost shouting down the phone. 'He thinks he's over a hundred years old and he can talk to the animals… yes… talk… like Dr Dolittle… talk… yes. He's mad… I'm staying in York overnight and I'll be back in the office tomorrow… Ok… bye for now.'

Denise was staying at a hotel on the A64 not far from the village where she had met with John Ryder and after a hard day's work all she wanted to do was relax, have a bath, something to eat and then bed, which was fortunate really because the hotel was only designed for a quick overnight stay and then back on the road.

On the small estate with the hotel was a 'McDonald's, her food for the night, a busy petrol garage, a Land Rover car dealership and a tractor dealership for some manufacturer she had never heard of before.

The joys of working away from home.

After taking the short walk to 'McDonalds's for something to eat, she made her way back to the hotel and flung herself onto the bed face down… at least the bed seemed nice.

She couldn't get John Ryder out of her head. How had he become so... so... mad? Probably because he had lived on his own for so long. A thought flashed through her head... why didn't she use her laptop to research him and the house Beckside.

'Good idea Denise,' she said out loud to herself as she leapt off the bed and grabbed her laptop from her bag.

She tried Googling John Ryder but that didn't work, so she searched for the village near York, which brought up all the village history and a few items on planning permission in the village but very little else. She scrolled down, again and again, page after page and accidentally landed on a small website by a local historian. It had many pictures taken over the years of the village, and its people, when all of a sudden there was a section marked Beckside. It was John Ryder's house. It was built as a wooden pig-shed originally, around 1900 and over the years it was knocked down and rebuilt until around 1913, when it largely resembled the house you see today. There was some text about its history and a picture of a young woman at the front door, but there were also pictures taken much later from the 60s and on into the 70s. There was a black and white picture of a man and his dog standing at the gates watching the local hunt go past, dated 1967... she had to look again and zoom the picture as far as she could... it was John Ryder and his dog... Jack. The picture looked exactly like them... like they are now.

Denise raised her head from looking at the laptop display and stared open-mouthed at the wall opposite.

NO WAY... NO WAY. It can't be? She called out.

Returning to the laptop, she clicked on the remaining pictures and there was only one more of John Ryder and Jack, and that was taken in 1972. John was in the field cutting bushes down and she could just make out Jack in the foreground sat watching.

Denise was confused. She stood up and began pacing up and down in her small bedroom. How could this be? It's not possible... but it must be... she had just seen the pictures and she had met him... he had told her and she didn't believe him.

Now what?

Now what indeed. She said out loud. I've got to go back and see him again.

She immediately picked up her phone and called Steve from work where it rang and rang for ages.

'Hello. Steve. It's Denise,' she said excitedly. 'And...' But she was interrupted mid-sentence.

'I can see it's you Denise, your name is showing on my phone... what's wrong.'

'Nothing, I wanted...'

'Nothing... then why are you ringing me at one in the morning?'

'1 o'clock ooh... sorry, I didn't realise... sorry. I just wanted to tell you I won't be back in the office tomorrow, there's something I want to do.' She said hoping he wouldn't ask what, because she would feel completely daft having to explain that John Ryder might be telling the truth.

'Ok... Now... Do you think I might get back to sleep?... Bye.' And he hung up.

Denise held the phone close to her chest for a few moments trying to get her head around what she was about to do tomorrow... and more to the point, if John Ryder would see her again after she had been so rude to him... what if he refused to see her?

I'll worry about that tomorrow.

Chapter 11

Denise was up early, partly because she wanted to get over to Beckside and see John Ryder again, but also because the curtains to her hotel room didn't fit the size of the window properly, so when the sun came up in the morning it shone directly into her room making everything so bright it was impossible to sleep.

After an invigorating shower, which made her feel alive and ready to tackle the day ahead, she got dressed and put her make-up on before driving the one hundred yards or so to 'McDonalds's to get her breakfast, which, after much deliberation, was just a coffee that she placed carefully in the cup holder in the middle of the car. She decided not to drink it there and then but to wait until she parked up at Beckside, where she could take her time drinking it and think about what she was going to say to John Ryder.

Denise parked her car on the side of the road, at the end of the track that led to Ryder's house, where she began to drink her coffee, which had cooled down nicely. She ran over different scenarios in her head again and again as to how to approach the weird situation that, given the facts, he appeared to be over one hundred years old, which she knew was crazy, but finally gave up and decided to just go and meet him again face to face … if he would talk to her after she was so rude to him yesterday.

The gates were shut and locked as usual so she tried peering through the cracks to see if he was around but he was nowhere to be seen.

There was only one thing for it.

'Hello. Mr Ryder... Hello.' She called out but there was no reply.

'Hello... Is there anyone there... Please, Mr Ryder, I'd like to talk to you. I'm sorry about yesterday.'

Nothing. No reply. Jack didn't even bark.

She was determined to talk to him, so after studying the huge gates and the fences on either side, she decided to try and find a way in. To the right of the double gates were two six-foot-high and six-foot-wide fence panels that bordered the field on the right-hand side of the house and looking closely it seemed possible to get round and through to the other side... only a couple of problems.

One... She would have to straddle the railings to the bridge and walk along a narrow ledge the full length of the two fence panels. She was glad she was wearing her trouser suit.

And two... Where the fence met the field was a six-foot high, three-foot wide hawthorn hedge bulging with two-inch long spikes that could pierce her skin in an instant, and the hedge ran the full length of the house.

Nothing an intrepid Yorkshire girl couldn't overcome.

It was more difficult than it looked if that was possible, and after about five minutes of balancing along the twelve-inch wide ledge that over-looked a ten-foot drop into the stream, and pushing and scrambling her way through the hawthorn hedge, she arrived victorious on the other side, looking only a little worse for wear with a few scratches to her arms and legs and her hair looking as if she'd been dragged through the hedge backwards.

She stood motionless for a few seconds relieved at concurring the obstacles... and to get her breath back. She then straightened her hair and brushed herself down to get rid of all of the leaves and twigs from her clothes to try and look at least half presentable before hopefully meeting with John Ryder again.

Now she was on the other side of the gates she could see so much more but he was still not around, so she slowly walked up to the front of the house and using the big brass knocker in the middle of the door she lifted it and let it fall twice. It was heavy so it sounded as if she had meant to bang the door hard… but she hadn't, and it made her feel a little self-conscious causing her to play nervously with her hands.

No-one came to the door, so rather than knock again and possibly risk offending him even more, she took a step to her right and cupping her hands to the window, she peered through hoping to see him but he was nowhere to be seen, so she did the same to the window on the other side of the door… again nothing.

Now what?

She walked across the front of the house and along the driveway which ran the full length of the house, trying to make her steps as quiet as possible which wasn't easy in extremely noisy gravel. As she approached the rear of the house she stopped and peered around the corner.

There he was, knelt on the patio, with Jack on one side and squirrels all around him, sat on their hind legs. They were looking at something he had in his hands which she couldn't quite see. Feeling brave, she took a step closer and immediately a huge flock of very hefty-looking crows took off from the large oak tree by the garage to her right. They made an enormous amount of noise which was directed straight at her as they flew over and around her causing her to shrink down in fear of being pecked.

John Ryder spun round along with Jack who ran towards her barking and the squirrels ran into the field looking for cover.

'Denise… what are you doing here?' He enquired calmly, gesturing with his empty hand to the crows to leave her alone. 'And how did you get in? Did I leave the gates open and unlocked… that's not like me?' he said with a mischievous grin on his face.

'No… sorry… I…' She stuttered feeling embarrassed at being caught.

'Don't worry… I knew you had got round the fence…'

'How… how did you know? I didn't see you.'

'I have spies everywhere… look.' He said pointing to a Kestrel hovering about fifty feet in the air above them.

'What… you mean…'

'Yes… she told me you were coming.'

'She?'

'Yes. She has a nest in the Ash tree over there… and she's hunting to feed her young.'

'Mr Ryder, I…'

'Call me John.'

'John. I…'

'Look… can whatever you wanted to talk to me about, wait a while, you see, I have an injured squirrel here.' He said opening his hand and showing her a baby squirrel with a broken back leg. 'I need to help him rather quickly as he's in a lot of pain.'

'I didn't know you were a vet?' Said Denise rolling her head to one side inquisitively.

'I'm not, but the animals come to me if they're injured or need help.'

'Oh yes, you talk to the animals don't you,' she replied sarcastically.

'Yes,' said John looking her straight in the eye.

'Oh… err… how can you mend its leg if you're not a vet?'

'Watch…' John turned away from her and started to walk into the field. 'Come on guys,' he said to the squirrels as they leapt in the air behind him in the long grass. 'Come on Denise… you'll love this.'

'Err… Ok… I'll follow behind you,' she said nervously not knowing what to expect. 'How can you mend a broken leg in a field?'

'You'll see…' he replied coming to a stop under the Yew tree in the middle where he knelt by the pond, brimming over with shimmering golden water.

Denise took a few steps into the field and then stopped to watch, expecting him to use a twig or a piece of wood to tie around the squirrel's leg.

She couldn't quite see what he was doing because of the way he was bent over so she took another couple of steps towards him. The glistening golden-coloured water of the small pond immediately came into view and she could see John holding the baby squirrel in the water. A confused look spread across her face because it was a very strange way to heal a broken bone, but then, as she was watching intently so as not to miss anything, John closed his eyes and tilted his head back as if to look into the canopy of the Yew tree overhead.

Within seconds, the pond began to glow a beautiful golden yellow, brighter and brighter until it almost became too intense to watch, and then as quickly as it had begun, it stopped. John brought his head forward and lifted the baby squirrel out of the water, wiping the water away with his hand. The squirrels all gathered around, in fact, there were so many of them, you could hardly see John. He gently opened his hand and let the young squirrel step onto the ground where it immediately ran to its parents. The squirrels clambered over John's entire body making him appear to be one swirling mass of fur and tails and then within a few seconds they were gone leaving him kneeling on the ground under the Yew tree. He smiled, slowly stood up and walked towards Denise who was frozen to the spot with her mouth open and a blank look on her face.

'You'd better close that before you catch a fly,' said John with a huge grin on his face.

'Wh... Wh... Wh...'

'What just happened?' John finished the sentence for her as she was shocked, dazed and a little confused. 'Well... honestly... I don't know, but what I do know is that whatever it is, it's here to help... for a good purpose. I've learnt how to make it work over the years because it only seems to work if I close my eyes and say a few words.'

Denise finally came to her senses and was full of awe and brimming with excitement at what she had just witnessed.

'That was amazing... incredible... wonderful... wait a minute... what words?'

'I sort of pray,' said John shrugging his shoulders slightly.

'What do you mean, sort of pray?'

'Well, I don't pray as you would pray to a god or the God, I just ask IT to help.'

John began to walk back across the field to his house and Denise spun round knowing she had just witnessed something incredible and had so many questions she didn't know which one to ask first.

'Err... IT... Who or what is IT? Where has IT come from? Who put IT there?'

'Woa... I know as much as you... but you must admit it is pretty amazing don't you think?'

'Yes it is... is that how you've been able to live so long...

using the water from the pond I mean?' She said following John back to the house where she grabbed him by the arm and made him turn to look at her.

'John… whatever that is,' she said waving her arm in the direction of the Yew tree. 'Tell me… is that how you've managed to live so long… you and Jack.'

He stood face to face with her and took hold of both her hands.

'Yes… but you can't tell anyone Denise.'

'Hang on John. You have the answer to eternal life and perfect health in a pond in your field and you don't want me to tell anyone… are you mad.'

'It's not as simple as that Denise,' he said letting go of one of her hands and taking her a step towards the water pump on the patio.

'You see this pump… It has a pipe from the pond directly to here but if I try and mend a broken bone, or cure a sick animal… here at the pump… it doesn't work. I think whatever gives the water its power is linked to where it is in the field and the Yew tree.'

Denise let go of his hand and turned away.

'What are you thinking?' Asked John but she didn't reply, she just stood facing the field. John sat down on the wooden bench where Jack came to join him, sitting on the patio between his legs.

'What's she doing?' Asked Jack looking up.

'I don't know. I think I've traumatized her showing her the pond and the tree.'

'You see, I told you not to tell anyone,' said Jack licking his front paw.

'I know. I know. You were right,' said John reaching down

and stroking Jack on the top of his head.

Denise swivelled round.

'Were you just talking to Jack?'

'Yes.'

'What did he say?'

'He said he told me not to tell anyone.'

Denise looked at Jack and smiled.

'He was right... I've decided we mustn't tell anyone.'

'Good... But hang on a minute, your company wants to flatten the field and build houses. What can I do?'

'Yes... Right... Ok... I'm just going to make a call,' she said pulling her mobile from her pocket and dialling Steve Dickinson. Almost immediately it was answered.

'Steve... Denise. We have to stop the build on the field at Beckside... why... err... I can't tell you but we have to stop it.' She stood with her phone pressed to her ear for ages nodding and shaking her head and then nodding some more before finally hanging up.

'I can't stop it John... I'm sorry... I can't stop it,' she said sounding a little distraught.

Chapter 12

'Steeeeve…' Pleaded Denise placing her hands on his desk in front of him and leaning forward to look him directly in the eye. 'We have to stop the building works planned for the field at Beckside.'

'Denise… We've been through this,' said Steve leaning back on his chair and playing with his pen. 'Unless you give me a solid reason, I can't even do a report for the guys upstairs, let alone recommend we cancel the project. You have to tell me why?'

Denise stood bolt upright and folded her arms with the biggest sulking look on her face you have ever seen.

'Don't look at me like that,' said Steve pointing his pen at her. 'It's not going to work.' He stood up pushing his chair backwards with the back of his knees. 'Look, Denise… I need facts… solid facts… I can't recommend we cancel because his dog is old enough to get a bus pass, the guy is over a hundred years old and he thinks he can talk to the animals… oh… and he performs miracles from time to time… It just won't work.'

Denise let her hands drop to her side and stamped around like a toddler having a tantrum. After stomping around the room for a few seconds she stopped motionless in front of the office window which looked directly on to the car park. A fox and her two cubs appeared from under the bushes in the well-manicured leafy borders and slowly trotted across the concrete, disappearing in some more bushes further along.

'Isn't nature beautiful?' She said quietly, not expecting an answer.

'What... Denise... Hello.'

She turned to face Steve and walked slowly over to his desk.

'Steve. How long have I worked here?'

'Err... I'm not sure.'

'I'll tell you. Eight years. Eight good years. I've enjoyed just about everything... the job, the people... it's been great... but I'm not going to watch this company destroy what's going on with Ryder in that field.'

'What are you saying?'

'I'm saying I'm going to leave. I'm handing in my resignation.'

'Denise, come on... don't be rash. Think about it. The company has done this sort of thing for years and you've never worried about it before.'

Denise walked up to Steve and stood so close, face to face, you couldn't put a piece of paper between them.

'Well Steve, maybe I should have, maybe we all should have.'

Steve took a step back feeling uncomfortable at being so close. It gave Denise enough room to spin round on the spot and walk out of the office in silence without even a glance behind her as she left.

She made her way out of the building and into the car park, where she stopped and took a long, deep breath wondering what on earth she had done. As she stood by the front door to the office block, she could just see the two fox cubs poking their noses out from under the bushes on the other side of the car park, so she slowly wandered over hoping not to scare them off. As she came within a few yards of them she crouched down and held out her hand as if she had something to offer them.

'Come on little ones... I won't hurt you,' she said softly. 'Come on.'

John Ryder immediately popped into her head making her forget what she was doing and whisked her away into a daydream as she remembered him fixing the broken leg of the squirrel. While her mind was away at Beckside, the fox cubs plucked up the courage to investigate what she had in her hand, rubbing their wet velvety noses against her fingers which instantly brought her back from her flight of fantasy. The sight of the cubs nuzzling her hand filled her heart and body with a kind of warmth she couldn't explain... now she knew what she had to do...

She was going back to Beckside to see John Ryder.

Chapter 13

What have I done? Denise thought to herself over and over again as she drove towards Beckside. I had a wonderful job and now I've gone and thrown it all away… for what? A man who thinks he's Dr Dolittle and a field in possibly the sleepiest village in the world, if not the galaxy.

Once off the dual carriageway, the road to Beckside was a typically narrow country lane with high hedges and sharp corners every hundred yards or so, which made the final leg of the journey very slow and frustrating, but it wasn't long before she was entering the village and turning down Bond Lane towards Church Lane where John Ryder lived. She had already made her up her mind that she was going to park right outside his house, unlike last time when she parked about two hundred yards away.

This time was different. What did she have to lose? Nothing. Her small car bumped and bounced along the pot-holed track to the house, creating so much dust behind her that it looked like a dust-storm had just passed through.

She pulled onto the small bridge and brought her car to a sudden stop right in front of the big wooden gates. Turning off the engine she slowly opened the driver's door and clambered out, forgetting how little room there was to open the car door due to the white railings on either side… but she managed it and slammed the door… on purpose, hoping John Ryder or Jack would hear the noise and come to the gates to let her in.

No such luck.

She stood at the gates for what seemed liked ages, but in reality was probably only for ten minutes or so, shouting and calling with no response.

Why can't he have a door bell or a mobile phone like any normal person? She said out loud in frustration. Then an idea hit her like a slap in the face.

He says he can talk to the animals, and they can talk to him… so why don't I ask an animal to tell him I'm here… but which animal… She looked around her, and although she could hear birds singing, and rustling in the bushes, there wasn't a single creature to be seen anywhere.

Why is there never an animal around when you need one?

The rustling turned out to be a bunch of cows in the field on the opposite side of the house, but even Denise knew they were no good because they couldn't get through the hedge… she needed an animal that could get round the back… there must be one somewhere.

Then… she saw one… it was a squirrel clambering down the horse chestnut tree on the other side of the fence opposite her. She was just about to say something when she stopped… what do you say to a squirrel? You can't say excuse me Mr Squirrel… what if it was a female… it might get quite offended and run away. It saw her and turned to make its way back up the tree so she had no option but to say something… and quickly before it disappeared.

'Err… excuse me. Would you tell Mr Ryder I'd like to have a word with him please?' She said in a very matter-of-fact way, feeling extremely silly, but the squirrel stopped, turned round and wiggled its nose at her before darting up the tree and becoming lost in the thousands of branches and leaves above them. Did the nose wiggle mean… Yes, of course, I'll let him know… or did it mean, what are you saying human, I don't understand a word... Now what?

She didn't have to wait long because Jack came running round from the back of the house and up the driveway, where he stopped and began sniffing at the cracks in the gates.

'Jack. Am I pleased to see you,' she said bending down to look at him through the gate. 'Go and tell Mr Ryder I'd like to have a word.'

'No need Denise,' came a voice from behind the gates. 'I'll let you in... hang on.'

She stood up as she could hear the rusty old bolt being slid back, and then the left-hand gate swung open.

'Hello,' said John with a smile.

'Hello,' she replied.

'Come in... Come in.'

'Thank you. Oh... what about my car?'

'It'll be fine, just leave it there. It won't be in the way. I never have visitors anyway.'

'Ok. Thank you.'

John shut the gate behind her and locked it as usual, which for some reason didn't make her feel in the slightest bit worried this time as she bent down to stroke Jack.

'So... what can I do for you Denise?' Asked John with a broad smile on his face.

'I... I... I know. Could we have some nettle tea, and I'll tell you all about it?'

'What a good idea,' said John looking up into the crystal blue sky. 'It's about eleven o'clock anyway.'

Denise tilted her head to one side as she looked at him.

'How do you know?' She said looking at her watch which told her it was ten past eleven.

'The sun,' he replied pointing into the sky as he gestured to her to follow him along the driveway so they could make their way round the back.

Just as they reached the Oak tree which was next to the garage, John turned towards her.

'That was very clever of you… earlier.'

'What was?' She said opening her eyes wide.

'Telling the squirrel to come and get me.'

'Oh…' She laughed as she straightened her long blonde hair. 'What did he say?'

John rocked his head back as he laughed a deep laugh.

'He said… there's a strange human woman at the gates… I immediately knew it was you.'

'How?'

'Well, who else could it be? I never have female visitors, so it had to be you. Please sit… I'll make us some tea.'

'Thank you,' she said sitting on the wooden bench. It was nice to be back she thought to herself as she looked around… it was so peaceful here.

It didn't seem to be more than a few minutes before John returned holding two mugs, one of which he handed to her.

'Careful… it's hot.'

'Ok… thanks. I've got it,' she replied putting it on the make-shift stone coffee table.

'So,' began John sitting down next to her and balancing his mug of tea on the arm of the bench. 'What do you want to talk to me about?'

Denise was so nervous she couldn't help fiddling with her fingers on her lap.

'Well… the last time I was here you… and this place made such a huge impression on me… a massive impression. So much so… I went back to work and tried to persuade them not to build on your field.'

'That's brilliant Denise,' said John turning himself more towards her. 'Thank you.'

'Yes… but… they wouldn't listen… and I couldn't stop thinking about you healing the squirrel's leg… and the water… and the Yew tree.'

'They have that effect on you don't they,' Interrupted John with a huge smile on his face.

'Yes… So I gave up my job. I resigned.'

'Why?'

'I'm not sure. I've never done anything like that before… I think… it's because I couldn't make them understand how wonderful and special this place is… and you… and Jack. For goodness sake John…' She said waving her hands around in the air. 'You're over a hundred, Jack's a geriatric, what, over seventy, and you and the animals talk to each other… how much more special do you need?'

John laughed out loud.

'Don't forget the healing of the animals.'

'Oh yes, and you use magic water to heal the animals.'

John reached over and took hold of Denise's left hand as she reached down with her other hand and picked up her cup of tea, blowing over its surface before taking a sip.

'Wow… what is this? It's not the same tea as before?' She exclaimed in delight.

'Oh… it's a blend of nettle and mint… it's good isn't it.'

'It's lovely… you see… this place is wonderful. It's so peaceful.'

'I know, you don't have to tell me, why do you think I've stayed here for so long?'

Denise took another sip of her tea and put it back on the table before putting her hand on top of John's.

'I suppose another reason for resigning was so I could help you... here.'

John was a bit surprised by her question leaning back a little before replying.

'Help with what?'

'Oh... no... yes... I mean... help you fight against the company that's going to try and build on the field.'

'Oh. I see. Yes. That's a good idea.'

'Yes. I thought so too,' she said as a huge smile crept across her face.

John looked into her eyes for what seemed like an age and then let go of her hands to stand up.

'I've had an idea Denise... I mean... what if...' he stopped and paused for a second.

'What if... what?' Asked Denise leaning forward on the bench.

John spun round just as Jack jumped up onto the bench next to Denise.

'I've lived here for... well, for so long, I can hardly remember how long and it's about time Jack and I had some human company. This is a big house. It has so many rooms I can't remember the last time I went into some of them... you can take your pick of the spare bedrooms... why don't you stay here?'

'What?... Err... I don't know. I mean... I have my own place, a flat, and I hardly know you,' she said shocked and surprised at John's offer, leaning over to one side slightly and stroking Jack's head.

'Yes, you're right... you're right. I'm sorry for asking you... I feel silly. I should never have asked you.'

Denise jumped up and stood directly in front of John leaving just enough gap between them that was normal for people who had only just met… but felt like they had known each for ages.

'No… I would love to,' she said as the pair of them felt the biggest smiles spread across their faces. 'I don't have a job any more and I could leave my flat for a while.'

'Good,' replied John.

'Good,' said Jack to John looking up at him from the bench.

'Did Jack just say something?' Said Denise smiling down at Jack.

'Hahaha… Yes. He said Good too.'

Chapter 14

It's now been a couple of weeks since Denise decided to stay at Beckside with John and Jack and, to put it mildly, it's been an eye-opener for her. She knew John could understand the animals but she didn't realise and appreciate when he said they talked to him, and he to them, how true it was. She witnessed animals of all different sizes, shapes and species literally hold lengthy conversations with him... or so she thought. She could hear John talking to them and replying as if they were talking or asking him a question... but she couldn't hear them speaking... at all... so always in the back of her mind, there was a little bit of doubt rolling around... could he hear them and talk to them... or was he as mad as a cat in a bath of water?

She had noticed something he did every day which was playing on her mind and finally plucked up the courage to ask him about it.

'John...' she said softly as she walked out into the back garden where he was sitting on the bench. 'Do you mind if I ask you a question?'

'Of course I don't mind,' he said getting up and stretching his arms into the air as he looked out into the field. 'What is it?'

'Well... you know how you talk to the animals... and I can't... I mean... how did you get the power... the whatsit... the thing that allowed you to understand them?'

'Ahh... I was wondering how long it would take you to get round to that question?' He said with a big cheesy grin on his face.

'Well... surely you can understand... I can't hear them... so it makes it difficult for me to believe you.'

'I know,' he said turning to look her straight in the eye. 'Would you like to be able to hear them too... the animals?'

'Well... yes... of course... who wouldn't?' She replied nervously.

'It's not as easy as that Denise... once they know they can talk to you... and you can understand them... they will ask you to help them... or they will offer to help you... animals are not like us... humans... if you break their trust you will lose them forever... no second chances.'

Denise was stunned at how serious John had become. In the relatively short time she had known him, he had always been light-hearted and made jokes about most things... but this... this was real... he meant it.

'Err... yes... yes,' she replied genuinely. 'I see you go into the field every morning and sit under the Yew tree... is that how you get... get the power... the thing?'

'Yes... it took me a while to work out that it wasn't just the water from the pond... it has to be drunk from the field and under the Yew tree. I had been taking handfuls of water from the pond to quench my thirst after I'd been working in the field and it was doing that, that allowed me to hear the animals. I piped the water to the pump there...' he gestured with this hand towards the pump on the patio and the pipework. 'But drinking that water alone doesn't work... it has something to do with where it is in the field... under the Yew tree... over there,' he said pointing towards the middle of the field.

'Let her do it John... go on,' came a voice from under the bench... it was Jack.

'How long have you been there?' Asked John as he bent down to see who it was.

'Has he said something?' Asked Denise bending down to look at Jack as well.

'Yes… He said I should let you do it.'

'Well. It's settled then. Let's do it… Oh… Will it hurt?' Said Denise nervously.

'Denise… it's water. All you have to do is drink it… but I must warn you it does taste a bit peculiar,' said John with a glint in his eye and a smile on his face.

'You…' she replied smiling and gently slapping his shoulder.

'Come on then, no time like the present,' said John taking hold of her hand and leading her into the field. As they approached the Yew tree Denise slowed down a little, tugging on his hand.

'What's wrong?' Asked John as he dropped her hand and took the extra couple of steps to reach the pond and the tree, where he dropped to his knees facing away from her. He cupped his hands together and scooped the water into his mouth again and again. She just stood behind him… watching… looking at all the animals and birds and insects all around them. They seemed to be waiting… waiting for her to take a drink which made her feel so nervous and self-conscious that she wanted to run away. John could sense there was something wrong.

'Denise don't worry. Everything will be Ok.'

'That's easy for you to say… you've been doing this for years.'

'I know… I know… but honestly… it will be Ok,' he said trying to reassure her. 'Look… if you don't want to, then that's fine as well. We can go back to the house and forget it.'

'No… No. I'm going to do this,' she said giving her

shoulders a huge shrug. 'Are the animals saying anything thing to you?' John looked around and saw them all making a huge circle around them, but amazingly there was no sound... at all.

'No... completely quiet.'

He took her hand as she knelt with him at the edge of the shimmering pond. In unison, they cupped their hands together and gulped the water down. Denise stopped and looked at all the animals that had now moved much closer and formed a crowd around them but she couldn't hear them talking or saying anything.

'It's not working. I can't hear them talking,' she said disappointedly

'Give it time Denise... give it time. Drink some more... go on.'

They both bent over and drank some more with John finishing off by splashing it all over his face.

'Ahhh... that feels good,' he said throwing his head back.

'It's still not working,' said Denise feeling completely downhearted and looking into her reflection in the rippling golden-coloured water.

'How do you know it's not working?'

'Because I can't hear any of the animals... none of them.'

'How do you know?'

She raised her head up and with one of those looks a woman can give a man when she means business she said in a loud, almost shouting type of voice.

'John... I can't hear them... all right,' but John had a bewildered look on his face.

'Den... I didn't say anything.'

She looked around her at all the animals, and right next to her was Jack.

'Was it you Jack?'

'Who else do you think would talk to you… none of this lot knows you yet?' Said Jack standing up from sitting next to her.

She threw her arms around him and gave him the best cuddle a human lady could give a talking dog.

'I can hear you Jack… I can hear you… you can hear me.'

'Yep… you bet.'

She let go of Jack and stood up making the, by now, huge crowd of animals leap a step back.

'Does that mean all the other animals can hear me… and I can hear them?'

'Yes,' said John. 'Although some animals are much more shy than others so it might be a while before they say anything to you.'

She became quite overwhelmed by the sight of the animals… there were so many, and so many different types. There was Jack, rabbits, mice, many, many mice and squirrels. She spotted the squirrel family that John helped previously, a couple of badgers, a fox and her cubs, birds… so many birds of every kind, even a tortoise.

'Hello everyone,' she called out, waving her hands at the same time. They all called out, 'Hello' in return together, putting a huge smile on her face.

John was right. Where was he? She swivelled round on the spot looking for him, where could he be? He was right by her side only a few moments ago.

Then she spotted him.

He was on the other side of the Yew tree standing in front of the most fantastic stag deer. It had brilliant white fur which seemed to shine and give off an almost golden glow like the sun. All the animals around her seemed to bow their heads a little and take a step back. John nodded his head to the deer and with a blink of an eye it was gone and he was walking back towards them.

'What was that?' She said almost speechless as to the beauty of what she had just seen.

'That was the White Hart of the forest. He came to wish us well and good fortune for the future. We should feel very honoured he appeared for us, he hardly ever shows himself... at all... to anyone.' He said smiling at her and taking her hands in his. 'Anyway... I told you the water would work... now you're just like me and Jack.'

'Yes... Err... Thank you. How often does that... the White Hart come here?'

'Oh... He's only ever been here a couple of times... he's very shy.'

'Why did his fur seem to glow?'

'It's a long story... but he sort of represents the quest for knowledge and legend has it that he can never be caught... oh and he's a bridge between this world and the next... and his friend is a unicorn.'

'What?'

'See... I told you it's a long story.'

'I... I...'

'Shall we go back to the house now you can talk to the animals...? Oh, I forgot to tell you.'

'Noooo... Why didn't you tell me before...? What is it? Don't tell me... I turn into a dragon... My hair falls out... Tell me.'

'If you want to keep talking to the animals you have to drink from the pond under the Yew tree everyday... otherwise... it stops, and you can't hear or talk to them again... or until you drink the water again… Ok.'

'Is that all… Phew… Yes, let's go and have a cup of tea… I need one after this… It's not every day a woman gets to talk to the animals and see a white deer who has a unicorn for a best friend.'

Chapter 15

Months have passed since John led Denise to the pond under the Yew tree to drink the water and she acquired the ability to hear and talk to the animals. She would be the first one to admit it hadn't been plain sailing, but all in all, she had now come to accept it, and all the good and bad things it brought to her life.

The good things are being able to listen to all the creature's problems, which are very much like our own, family issues, problems with the children, food and so on but the bad things, and thank goodness there aren't many of those, the bad things are when she or John can't help, in fact, only the other day a family of Wrens had come to see them. The poor things... they were almost starving until John and Denise were able to give them some food. The father Wren had always provided for them until a couple of days ago when he never returned after leaving the nest one morning. The mother had done as much as she could but there were just too many little mouths to feed so as a last resort she had come with her offspring to see John. They had heard that he might be able to help... and, as always, he did his best. Denise was talking to the mother Wren when she saw John near the front gates of the property beckoning her. She made her excuses to mother Wren and walked along the drive to where John was standing. He was nearly in tears.

'John... what's wrong?' Asked Denise knowing already she wasn't going to like the answer. He looked down at his hands that were cupped together and opened them slowly. There inside was father Wren... dead.

'Ooohhh nooo...' Denise said as quietly as she could to not let the family of Wrens hear. 'What happened? How did he die?' John took a second or two to answer.

'It looks like he had been impaled by a two-inch-long Hawthorne spike. It's gone right through his chest... look. It probably happened when he flew into the hedge looking for food.' He whispered as he turned the Wren's little body over to show Denise who recoiled in horror at the sight of it.

'Poor father Wren,' she said with tears forming in her eyes. 'Oh no, what about the family?'

'I know. Don't worry I'll go and tell them,' said John as he started to walk back to where the family of Wren's were eating some berries he kept to hand for just this kind of emergency. He was always the one that told the animals the bad news... he had done it for so many years, and besides, he felt it was his duty.

Denise had so much admiration for him because she knew how much he loved and cared for these beautiful creatures.

So there... the good times and the bad times. But today was going to turn into one of the worst days for a very long time.

'John... John,' Shouted Jack as he bounced across the field. He might be over seventy years old but he could still put on a burst of speed when he had to.

'What?' Replied John calmly without even looking up from doing a bit of weeding in the vegetable patch at the back of the house.

'John... some men are here.'

'Ok... give me a minute... I'll just...'

'John... now... come quickly,' said Jack skidding to a halt

and throwing up clouds of dust and soil in front of where John was weeding.

'Jack...' cried out John as he stood up to avoid breathing in the dust while he was straddled across the lettuces and the carrots. 'What's the hurry, they can't get in. I'll go and open the gate.'

Jack lifted his front paws and rested them on John's knees straining his head back to look up.

'John... they're not at the gate... they found their way over the old bridge in the corner... they're in the field... with Denise... quick.'

John didn't need to be told twice. He threw down his trowel and within a couple of strides had cleared the vegetables and was into the field. He could see two men dressed in suits, both wearing high-vis waistcoats. One was carrying a tall, at least six-foot, red and white measuring stick and the other had just stretched out the legs of a tripod with what looked like a theodolite on top. They were a good hundred yards away over in the far corner of the field. Denise had grabbed their measuring stick and was trying to wrestle it out of the man's hands when he gave it a strong jerk back and then forward. It caught her on her shoulder and sent her falling back onto the grass.

Seeing what had just happened, John wasn't going to stand by and watch them hit Denise.

'What's he doing?' Said the younger of the two men holding onto the measuring stick.

'Not sure...' replied the other. 'But he's far enough away not to bother us at the moment.'

John threw his head back and raised his arms into the air with open hands.

'Now what's the idiot doing?' Said the man holding the tripod.

'Haha. Looks like he's going to do a rain dance,' replied the other laughing out loud.

Denise got to her feet and was as confused as the two men as to what John was doing. This was all new to her, she had never seen him do this before. She watched him swirl his arms around his head and then rapidly brought them down pointing directly at the men.

'Now he's pointing at us... Haha... oohh... quick... let's run... NOT.' Said one of the men mockingly.

The leaves and branches on the trees along the edge of the field and behind the house began to shake and within seconds the sky became as dark as night. It was thick with birds... thousands of them. Crows, Ravens, Starlings... too many to count.

'What the...' cried one of the men, while they both stood watching in awe as the birds swirled above their heads.

While the men were distracted watching the sky, Denise slowly moved away and back towards John, but she was just as amazed and scared as the men were.

Then without any warning the huge mass of birds compacted together into what looked like a huge spear and dived down, straight at the two men. They grabbed their equipment and ran as fast as they could towards the wooden bridge in the corner of the field. They were too slow, and the sound of birds hitting human bodies could be heard one after another along with cries and shrieks of pain from the men. They managed to scramble through the bushes and over the bridge, out into the adjacent field where they stumbled and staggered back onto the track outside the house. They could be seen running back in the direction of the road at the end of the track where their car must have been parked.

The huge swirling black cloud of birds circled above John's

house extending from one horizon to another. They appeared to hover above for a few seconds as if waiting for a command... and then as quickly as they appeared, one by one they landed in the trees, and daylight and normality were restored.

Denise walked slowly up to John and threw her hands around his waist laying her head on his shoulders. Tears started to stream down her face which John wiped away with his soil-covered hand.

'We can't let them build here John... not after that. You... and this place are special.'

'I know,' whispered John. 'I know.'

Chapter 16

'What on earth happened to you two?' Enquired Steve Dickinson leaning back into his high-backed leather office chair, 'you look like you've been in a fight.'

'You might well ask,' replied Phil Watson, one of the two surveyors that had just returned from the field at Beckside. 'We've just got back from John Ryder's place. Remember... the survey you asked us to do... well...'

'Yes... well...' interrupted John Kirby, the second and less senior of the two surveyors. 'Next time kindly ask someone else.'

'Why... what happened guys?' Said Steve Dickinson standing up to raise the blind on his window and allow more light to fall on the two rather-dishevelled surveyors. 'Blimey, you really have been in the wars... what was it... a group of angry protesters?'

'To start with it was your friend... what's her name... Denise.' Began Phil Watson. 'Then... then...' he stopped and looked across at John Kirby who quickly returned his look with a shrug of his shoulders.

'Hang on...' said Steve walking round his desk towards the two surveyors. 'Denise was there?... But surely she didn't do this to you guys?' He said gesturing with his hands at their ripped and blooded clothes.

'No... yes... well... no,' said Liam lowering his eyes towards the floor.

'Which one is it guys... yes or no?'

'Nn... no,' stuttered Phil. 'Although she did grab the two-metre measure and Liam tried to grab it... which unfortunately... accidentally... knocked her to the ground.'

Steve's eyes opened wide in dismay and his eyebrows seemed to move to the top of his head, just beneath his rather receding hairline. He threw his arms into the air and turned to face the window... if steam could have come out of his ears, now was the time it would have happened. He stood motionless and completely silent for a couple of seconds before turning to face the two surveyors.

'Please don't tell me we are now going to have a lawsuit on our hands guys... that's the last thing this company needs right now.'

Both Phil and Liam looked at each other before Phil spoke up.

'No. I'm sure nothing like that is going to happen Steve. Look at us... I'm sure if they did we would have far more of a case against them.'

'Them... who is them?'

'Oh... Denise and the owner of Beckside... John Ryder. He was there as well. It was him who did this to us... well not directly... but he was the one that instigated it.'

'Did he attack you guys?'

'No... but... he made the birds attack us.' As soon as Phil said the sentence he knew it was going to be hard work explaining what had happened.

'Birds... did you just say... birds?'

'Err... yes. He made thousands of birds attack us which meant we had to run for our lives,' said Phil looking at Liam as both of them nodded in agreement.

'Are you telling me that John Ryder made birds attack you?'

'Yes... thousands of them,' replied Liam.

'How... how did he make thousands of birds attack you? Did anyone else see this?'

'Well... no... yes... Denise saw... obviously... she was in the field.'

'Oh yes, you had knocked her onto the ground because she grabbed hold of your ruler... stick... measuring thing.'

'Yes... no... she had got up by that time and was standing watching.'

'So the birds attacked you and didn't bother with Denise.'

'Yes... yes. I told you,' said Phil feeling less confident by the second and wishing they hadn't gone into the office to explain. 'John Ryder stood in the field and directed the birds to attack us, which as you can see, they did, and we ran back to the car, at which point the birds disappeared... went away... somewhere, and we came straight back here.'

Steve Dickinson stood for a moment playing with his hands.

'The contract to build the houses on that field is too lucrative to lose... so I will have to think of something else... thank you guys... go and get cleaned up.'

Phil and Liam didn't need to be told twice so they immediately turned and left the office, leaving Steve pondering what to do next. After a few minutes of pacing up and down, he concluded. The only thing to do was what he had done many times before, and that was to be a bit more hands-on... after all, John Ryder didn't own the field, in effect he was just a squatter.

Chapter 17

It was late summer and as it happens sometimes in the UK, the evening had come in quite chilly, so John decided to light the large open fire in the living room. It took a while to get going but it was worth it... there's nothing more relaxing and cosy than a roaring open fire, so after a late dinner of vegetable stew and homemade bread, they both sat down in the living room to finally relax. It had been a busy day.

First thing in the morning there had been a problem with the waste water not running into the septic tank so a good few hours had been spent using the drain rods to clear a blockage. It sounds straight-forward but the manhole, which is in the field, was completely overgrown with grass and weeds and took some time to clear and lift. Also, the drain pipe into the septic tank is about one hundred and fifty feet long so pushing the rods along the pipe for that kind of distance wasn't easy, especially when John had to push the rods from the tank end. He didn't want whatever was blocking the pipe to fall into the tank... but he managed it with some help from Denise, who, considering she was a city girl and had never done anything like it before, performed remarkably well... even if she did hate getting her hands coated in... well... human poo. The blockage turned out to be about three feet of soil which had accumulated over time and grass had rooted, causing it to remain where it was in the pipe rather than be washed along into the tank. John wasn't surprised as it was a regular thing... well... regularly about every ten years, which meant he had cleaned the pipe out many times over the years.

After they had cleared the blockage and got cleaned up, they had a wonderful lunch of salad from the garden and a glass of homemade beer each, but lunch didn't last long unfortunately.

A huge swarm of bees moved slowly around the house, obviously looking for a place to land and make their nest. The trouble was they almost scared lunch out of Denise in the process because as a city girl, she had never experienced the sight of a large mass of bees swarming.

She was running around in a panic but John had seen this before and stood motionless in their path. He faced the swarm head-on with a smile on his face and closed his eyes. He had learnt over the years that he could communicate with bees if he listened carefully because they didn't talk with one voice. It was as if ten thousand people were speaking at the same time and they were all saying the same thing but all at slightly times so it sounded just like a noise… but if he listened hard, he could make out what they were saying They were just in a slight panic… all they wanted to do was land and make a new nest so he spoke slowly and gently, explaining there was a lovely Ash tree about thirty yards away which would make an ideal home. All the bees could hear his soothing voice and were drawn towards him, swarming all around him, which scared the living daylights out of Denise. After a few moments of listening to what John was saying they moved slowly away towards the large Ash tree at the far end of the garden where they gradually all clumped together and made their nest about fifty feet off the ground well away from prying eyes.

Sometime later there was another problem… it all happens at Beckside. Isn't there a saying from somewhere that everything happens in threes? Well, if it's not a saying, it should be, because it certainly happened in threes today. John and Denise were sitting on the wooden bench in the back garden when all of a sudden a small bird flew past them, probably only three feet away, followed by another much larger bird obviously in pursuit. They flew around and around with the bird in front frantically trying to escape from the much larger bird chasing it. John jumped to his feet and held out his hand instantly catching the smaller bird and causing the larger bird to swerve to avoid colliding into him. He cupped the small bird in both hands and whistled a high-pitched note over and over again which seemed to calm down the large bird who landed in a flurry of feathers and flapping of wings on the patio beside him. John beckoned to Denise to come towards him and opened his hands. Inside was a small colourful bird obviously scared. It was a chaffinch. He handed it to Denise who began to talk to it, calming it down and reassuring it that everything was going to be all right. John in the meantime had bent down and was in deep conversation with the larger bird, who after a few minutes, jumped onto John's hand and then flew up into the sky and away. He took the small chaffinch from Denise and assured it that it would never be chased by the sparrow hawk again, at least, not here at Beckside. He opened the palm of his hand flat, and the small bird flew away after dancing around on the top of John's head. Yet again Denise was flabbergasted at what had just happened.

There were still so many things that amazed her at John's house.

Anyway, back to the living room with John and Denise sitting in front of the roaring open fire.

John was sat on the sofa with his legs stretched out and resting on half of the pouffe stool, this way Denise could use the other half to rest her legs, but tonight she was scrunched up in the corner leaning against the arm of the sofa cradling a cup of mint tea in her hands.

'John, can I ask you a question?'

'Of course.' he replied without opening his eyes.

'When... I mean how long was it after moving here, did you realise that the water and the Yew tree were helping you and Jack to live longer?' John opened his eyes and shuffled himself up the sofa, putting both his feet on the floor.

'That's a difficult one Denise. Err... I'm not sure really... I've lived here so long now... I think it was probably after I had cleared the overgrown vegetation from around the Yew tree,' he pushed himself up onto his feet and stood in front of the fire warming his hands. 'I had been here for some years by then... and... well...' He stopped talking, walked over to the living room door and sneaked a look at Jack laid in his bed. 'It's all right,' he whispered. 'He's fast asleep.' Shutting the door quietly. Denise shuffled herself about on the sofa and put her feet on the floor.

'Why does it matter that Jack's asleep?' She asked sounding a little confused.

'As I was saying,' continued John now with his back to the fire. 'It wasn't long after I'd cleared the brambles from the Yew tree when it suddenly hit me...' He turned his head to check the door. 'Jack... well... he must have been old, very old, but he ran around like a pup... normally a dog of his age would have died by then.' John stopped and took a deep breath... Jack was more than a dog to him, he was like a member of the family, more than that even...a soul mate. 'That's why I shut the door, I didn't want him to hear that.'

'Oh... yes... I understand... of course,' said Denise listening intensely.

'And then as more years went by it was obvious that something weird was going on, because I wasn't getting any older either... Although I did learn early on that the water from the pump I installed has only limited effect, the real power comes from the pond and the Yew tree together.'

'So... what if you stopped drinking the water?'

'Ha... now there's a question?'

'Well...' said Denise pressing for an answer.

'Well...the real answer is... I don't know.'

'You don't know? But John we need to find out... what it... what if...'

'Don't you think I've thought about this Denise... for years? What if the water in the pond dries up? What if the Yew tree dies... what if... what if... too many what ifs... so now I just get on with my life and I've stopped worrying about things I can't control... you die if you worry, you die if you don't.'

'Yes but...' said Denise sounding a little worried.

'But what? The only way I can test what happens is to stop drinking the water, and I don't think that would be a good idea... do you?' John moved away from the fire and knelt in front of Denise. 'I was a little anxious about asking you to stay here with me Den... I'd been on my own for so long I didn't know how I... or Jack would react, but it's been wonderful having you here... and don't forget, you've been drinking the water from under the Yew tree as well.'

'Oh my God,' she cried jumping to her feet and nearly kneeing John in the face. 'You're right.' She walked round the room frantically mumbling to herself. John stood up and stopped her pacing about by taking her hands in his.

'But... I don't feel any different,' she said looking John

straight in his eyes.

'Neither do I Den, I never have. I'm over a hundred and don't feel any older than I did when I was twenty-one… apart from maybe a few more aches and pains… but otherwise, the same.'

'Yes… but… but now it's happening to me.'

'Yes… and think about it Den… we can grow old… very old… together… here at Beckside.'

'Yes, that's fantastic John… but have you forgotten something?' She said letting go of his hands and turning away.

'What?'

She turned to face him with tears in her eyes.

'John… they want to trash the field and build houses on it… we have to stop them.'

'I know… I know…'

'And another thing… if they succeed… the Yew tree and the pond will be gone… I'm OK because I've only drunk the water for a few months… but you… you and Jack… Oh John… I'm scared.'

John wrapped his hands around her waist and pulled her close, close enough to rest her head on his chest.

'I'm scared too Den… for the animals… for Jack… and for me and you, but there's nothing I can do… let's wait and see.' He gently pushed her forward so he could look into her teary eyes. 'Maybe… just maybe they will never come and they will forget all about us.'

Denise smiled up at him knowing full well, deep inside, that they would come and it was only a matter of when.

Chapter 18

Time passes as is the order of the universe and weeks go by without anything out-of-the-ordinary happening, that is, for Beckside. Of course, there are the usual things like everyday chores, caring for the vegetable patches and helping the animals when they came calling, which seemed to be getting more and more frequent... but that was probably because there were now more animals that knew about John, and Denise, and how they could help. There didn't seem to be a day that went by without some animal needing assistance of one kind or another, take today for example, John was minding his own business and relaxing having a cup of nettle tea at the wooden bench in the back garden when a badger limped into the garden with a large thorn in his front paw. John promptly pulled it out, washed it down and sent her on her way. It couldn't have been any more than ten minutes later when a whole flock of pigeons landed, in an awful lot of flapping of wings, on the patio. Earlier they had seen what they thought was some grain to eat lying in the road in the village, but it was some workmen resurfacing the lane with stones, sand and hot tar. They landed on the tar and now needed John to help with their burnt feet... which of course he helped as best he could, and again washed their feet down with some water from the pump and sent them flying off to find some real grain to eat this time.

Denise loved to watch John deal with the animals. He did it so easily, with so much care and attention... and love. She hardly ever got asked by the animals to help, they always went straight to John, and if they did ask her it was only because John was busy with something else and they couldn't wait. Anyway, she didn't mind… she wasn't as good as John… he'd been doing it so much longer… much, much, longer.

Denise was standing in the field watching the world, and the animals, go by, while John was still sitting on the bench when it happened…

'John… John…' Shouted Denise as loud as she could at the same time as running towards the corner of the field where the old bridge was. 'They're here… Quick.'
 John jumped to his feet and immediately followed. This was the moment he's been dreading.
 'Be careful,' he called after her as she sprinted to try and stop them getting into the field, but she was too slow. By the time she had seen them on the bridge, they were already only seconds away from entering the field. There was about twenty or more, all with axes and scythes, and at the rear, a huge tractor with a bulldozer blade on the front. She screamed at them.
 'GET OUT… GET OUT…GET OFF OUR LAND.'
 They all stopped, except for the tractor, which continued to move slowly up the field. A tall thin man wearing a suit, a high-vis waistcoat and a bright red hard hat, in front of the group, called back at Denise who had also stopped and was now joined by John and Jack.
 'BUT IT'S NOT YOUR LAND… Is it… Mr Ryder.?'
 'No…' replied John taking a step towards him. 'But I never said it was.' The suited man took a step towards John leaving only a few feet between then.

'That means Mr Ryder, you are trespassing. My client owns this land and has been granted permission to develop it for housing... so if you don't mind, make way and let my men do their job.' Denise lunged forward as if to strike the man but John caught hold of her arm and pulled her back.

'Don't Den... we can do this another way,' He said nodding at her, although she returned the look with a rather blank expression.

'The birds.'

He nodded again.

'Ah... the birds,' now she understood.

They let the men walk past them and then John looked into the trees and raised his arms in the air. Some of the workmen saw what he was doing and began to laugh and mock him, but it all too soon became evident what he was doing as the trees began to rustle and thousands of birds took to the air almost blocking out the light from the sun completely and turning day to twilight. The birds swooped down in one big mass, smashing into the men's bodies and the hard hats on their heads making such a clattering noise, that along with their shouts and screams, they could be heard hundreds of yards away on the main street of the village. The birds swirled around the workmen and the tractor like a swarm of bees or wasps attacking a predator, making it almost impossible to see who or what was underneath. One workman began to swing his axe at the birds killing half a dozen with one swipe, which he did again and again. Each time he hit the birds, their cries of pain fell on John's ears like the screams of men dying in battle. The other workmen saw what their colleague was doing and they did the same, swinging and hitting the birds, killing and stopping as many as they could. John fell to his knees clasping his hands over his ears.

'STOP...' he screamed. 'I CAN'T TAKE IT ANY MORE... STOP.' He jumped to his feet and began waving his arms wildly in the air. The birds instantly stopped their attack, circling above them and waiting for a call from John as to what to do next. Denise had run towards the Yew tree where the tractor was but she was too late and it ploughed into its trunk pulling its long roots out of the ground with ease. With one final push, the tractor toppled the Yew tree leaving it up-ended in the middle of the field. John put his hands over his eyes before raising them in the air signalling to the mass of birds to return to the trees, which they did.

'JOHN... JOHN,' called Denise as she tried in vain to lift the Yew tree back onto its base.

'Forget it Den... it's over.'

Denise fell to her knees as did John.

The workmen looked at the man in the suit. He looked around and realising they had made their point, gave the word for everyone to return to the vehicles and leave.

As the workmen made their way back to the old bridge something flashed in John's head... a thought... where was Jack? He'd been by his side when all this mayhem kicked off... where was he?

'DEN,' he called. 'HAVE YOU SEEN JACK?' She gave a fleeting look around but couldn't see him anywhere.

'NO.'

'JACK... JACK... WHERE ARE YOU?'

Nothing.

One of the workmen waved his arms about and then pointed in the direction of the toppled Yew tree.

'He went that way mate.'

John turned to look at the fallen Yew tree and immediately

knew something terrible had happened. His insides felt as if they were being tied into a huge knot and flipped inside out.

He felt sick.

He started to run towards the tree as Denise, who had heard what the workman had said, frantically began to search around looking for Jack.

'I can't see him… I can't… he's not here John.'

'Keep looking.' Said John panting as he reached the tree.

By this time, the workmen had all stopped what they were doing and were watching John and Denise's frantic search for Jack. The driver of the tractor was now standing next to them.

'Shall I move the tree with the tractor?' He asked, feeling awful that he might have hurt, or worse, killed their dog.

'No… No… If Jack's underneath it might do more harm than good.' Cried John bent double trying to see under the trunk of the tree.

'JOHN… JOHN.' Yelled Denise from around the other side near the large tangle of thick roots. 'HE'S HERE… I've found him.'

John scrambled around the tree to where Denise was knelt down rocking back and forth. She was sobbing loudly.

'What… wha…' He tried to speak but the words wouldn't come out. He could see a tail… a brown and white tail sticking out from under the Yew tree. He fell to his knees as he reached out to touch it. It was Jack. Denise threw her arms around John, unable to speak through her sobs and tears as he took hold of her and hugged her tightly for a second before pushing her away and jumping to his feet.

'No… no…I won't let this happen,' he said as he put his shoulder to the tree's trunk and tried to lift it but it was too heavy. He turned around and put his back to the trunk trying to lift it using his legs but it still wouldn't budge.

'HEY... GUYS... GIVE US A HAND.' Came a cry from behind him. It was the tractor driver. He had called to the other workmen to come and help lift the tree. They all dropped their tools and within only a couple of seconds there must have been fifteen strong workmen gathered on either side of the tree, all willing to help.

'After three,' called the driver. 'One... two... three... lift.' They all strained together and the Yew tree lifted about a foot in the air, just enough for John to reach under and scoop Jack up, pulling him clear in time for the men to drop the tree with a dull thud onto the ground.

John cradled Jack in his hands as everyone gathered around.

'Is he Ok?' Asked Denise still crying. 'John?'

But John knew Jack was dead as he cradled him in his arms and didn't reply. He bent his head forward and rubbed his cheek on Jack's hairy belly.

'I'm so sorry Jack...so, so sorry,' he sobbed.

'Give him room guys,' said the tractor driver holding out his arms to stop them getting too close to John as he moved a few steps away from the crowd. Denise's eyes were so full of tears she could hardly see where she was going as she took hold of John's arm... then... like a bolt of electricity through her brain, she had a thought.

'John...what if you heal him... heal him like all the other animals you heal,' she said so excited she was almost jumping up and down but John was so lost in his grief he didn't hear her. 'John... listen to me... heal him... like the others,' she said more aggressively and took hold of his shoulders to make him look at her. He lifted his head and stared into her eyes for a second or two.

'Den... he's dead. I've never brought an animal back from the dead... and besides... look around you... the Yew tree has been knocked over and the water in the pond has gone.' She stood motionless for a moment then ran over to where the pond had been. It had been filled in by all the soil from the roots of the trees so she knelt down and began to scoop out the mud. As she removed the soil, the small hollow began to fill with water... only this time it was a normal colour, not the golden yellow it had been. The workmen were now gathered around her wondering what she was doing as she stood up and pushed them back, asking them to give John room.

'Give him room? For what?' Asked one of them.

'You'll see,' she said as she called over to John and pushed the men back at least ten yards.

'John... John... come on... you have to try.'

'Yes... yes... of course,' he said obviously confused and walking over to the muddy hollow on the ground that was now about six inches deep with water. He knelt and laid Jack between his knees as he cupped the water in his hands and dripped it onto Jack's face and body. He did it again and again but nothing happened.

You could hear a pin drop as all the men and Denise watched what he was doing. They were all completely unaware of the animals that were gathering around them until one of the workmen noticed.

'Hey guys... look... look at this lot,' he said waving his hands in the direction of the animals who had gathered in the clearing between them and where John and Denise were by the toppled Yew tree.

John was beginning to panic because nothing seemed to be working so he gently picked up Jack's limp litte body and held him close to his chest.

'John... what are you doing?' Asked Denise quietly. She had never seen him do this before.

He wrapped his arms around Jack and holding him tightly to his chest he leaned forward so much his head touched the mud. With his forehead touching the ground he seemed to expel every bit of air from his lungs in the longest sigh Denise had ever heard. Heavy, dark clouds began to accumulate overhead followed by a swirling cold wind which made the trees and bushes shake and rustle.

'What's going on?' said one of the workmen holding onto his hard hat.

It's always been said that animals can sense danger and today was no exception. They had been so curious about John and Jack that they had formed a tight circle around them only a few feet away but now they began to move back, slowly at first, taking a step back... and then another... and just as a massive bolt of lightning landed in the field opposite leaving a blackened circle of charred grass and soil, all of them turned and ran in every direction seeking shelter wherever they could. The workmen were holding onto their hats and bracing themselves against the strengthening wind, too enthralled in what John was doing to leave. Denise was also beginning to get scared as she stood behind John looking up at the mass of swirling black clouds, now directly above them.

'JOHN,' she called leaning against the almost tornado-strength winds. 'WHAT'S HAPPENING?'

But there was no reply and she became more frightened... for John now, not the storm.

Was he all right? He hadn't moved for some time.

The wind was so strong, swirling around them... but John

seemed to be at its centre, almost untouched by the hurricane-like winds and as Denise battled against the force of the wind to get close to John, one of the workmen shouted.

'LOOK... LOOK... IN HIS ARMS.'

John's arms were crossed over his chest and he was bent over with his head touching the ground, almost completely hiding Jack from view but it was just possible to make out a dim glow which was growing in brightness coming from under his arms. As the glow became brighter and brighter, it was now the workmen's turn to feel afraid and they all took a couple of steps back, worried as to what was about to happen. A small patch of light appeared on John's back which very quickly grew in size and intensity until all of a sudden a huge golden shaft of light shot directly up into the centre of the swirling clouds turning them a deep red colour like a thousand autumn sunsets had come at once.

The workmen ran back towards the old bridge at the far end of the field crying out like little children as they ran...

'What's happening?'

'What's going on?'

'Who the hell is he?'

They all stopped at the field edge and turned to look back still curious but afraid of what they were witnessing. It was like something from a science fiction film.

'JOHN,' screamed Denise over the noise of the swirling wind. 'PLEASE SAY SOMETHING.'

But still he didn't respond.

Suddenly there was a huge flash of a bright, white light in every direction, but strangely no noise, and everything in a radius of about fifty yards was thrown backwards by the force of the blast causing Denise to end up flat on her back with her hair stretched back as if she had been hit by a sonic explosion of some kind. The workmen had to brace themselves against the explosion and all the trees and bushes were bent backwards away from the centre of the field.

There wasn't a bird or animal in sight.

The tornado of winds instantly stopped and as if brushed aside by the hand of... a higher being, the clouds were pushed away to reveal a glorious blue sky.

Denise struggled to her feet.

'JOHN...JOHN,' she cried as she half ran, half stumbled towards him. He was still in the same motionless position clutching Jack in his arms and leaning forward with his head touching the muddy ground. She was so scared as she approached him after witnessing what had just happened... what if he was hurt... or worse. She slowly reached out her hand to touch his shoulder trying not to startle him and as soon as her fingers made contact, she could see Jack's tail wiggle... just a little at first... then a bit more... then a really big shake followed by Jack falling out of John's grasp onto the ground where he stood and shook his little body like all dogs do after a bath. She reached towards him and took his head in her hands.

'Jack... you're alive... you're alive,' she sobbed at him with her eyes so full of tears she could hardly see.

'What happened... the last thing I remember is shouting at the workmen?' he said nodding his head towards the tractor as a cheer could be heard from the workmen at the bottom of the field. 'What are they cheering about?'

Denise had a soggy smile from ear to ear and rubbed the top of his head.

'It's a long story.'

Her attention was then quickly snapped back to John... he hadn't moved and was still crouched on the ground next to them.

'Oh no… Jack… John hasn't moved since… since…' she stopped talking not wanting to make Jack feel guilty that John was in this predicament because he'd helped to bring Jack back…well… from the dead. She put her arms around his shoulders and pulled him back into an upright position where he just flopped onto his back looking up at the now completely clear blue sky. She pulled his legs round from under him and tried to make him as comfortable as she could while she caressed his face with her hands. His eyes were shut and there were no visible signs of life so she leaned forward and rested her head on his chest.

'Oh thank God,' she whispered relieved. 'I can hear his heart beating… John… John… can you hear me?' She said louder hoping to get a response… but nothing. 'John… are you all right. Answer me… please.' Jack began to lick John's face but there was still no response.

'What are we going to do Jack? He's the one that always does the healing… I don't know what to do?'

'Me neither Denise,' replied Jack in-between licks of his nose and cheeks. 'Maybe we should get him inside?'

'Good idea… I'll need some help,' she said trying to lift him but finding he was a dead weight and way beyond her strength. 'HEY,' she shouted at the workmen who were still milling around by the old bridge at the far end of the field. 'HEY… can someone give me a hand?'

They were all still in shock after what they had just witnessed and were too busy talking amongst themselves… apart from one.

'YES. I'll give you a hand,' he shouted back. It was the tractor driver. He ran as best he could over the uneven ground to where Denise had managed to get John propped up on the ground with her hands under his shoulders.

'Give me a lift inside would you?'

'Yes... of course. What's wrong with him?'

'I'm not sure. Did you see what happened?'

'Yes. I've never seen anything like it. How did he bring the dog back to life?'

'It's a long story I'm afraid. A story for another time. What's your name?' She said as they struggled to half lift, half drag John back to the house.

'Brian.'

'Hi Brian. Nice to meet you... I think... I'm Denise.'

'I... I'm really sorry for knocking down the tree and trapping the dog.'

He said bowing his head apologetically.

'Don't worry about it... it's happened now... we can't turn back time.'

Brian stopped in his tracks making Denise stop as well.

'He did...' He said nodding at John and then looking at Denise with amazement in his eyes.

'Yes you're right... he did didn't he,' she replied with a feeling of pride surging through her body.

'He needs a doctor...or an ambulance you know... he's not well.'

'Let's get him inside. We don't have a phone here...or a mobile. Let me see how he is.' Between them, they managed to shuffle their way into the house and lift John onto his bed where Jack immediately jumped up and began licking his face again.

'Not bad for a seventy-something-year-old dog... jumping up like that,' said Denise without thinking.

'Seventy years old?' Said Brian sounding confused.

'Another long story Brian... don't worry about it.'

'After what I've seen today Denise, nothing surprises me

about this place,' he said shrugging his shoulders and walking out of the bedroom. 'I'll leave you to it, I've got to get back to the others.'

'Thank you Brian,' she called out after him.

Brian left the house and wandered back into the middle of the field where the fallen Yew tree was and stood over the small hollow in the ground where the pond used to be. It was full of water a few inches deep so he knelt down and washed his hands without really looking at what he was doing. After washing his hands he stood up and signalled to the workmen at the bottom of the field that he was on his way. He glanced down and something caught his eye.

'That's unusual?' He said out loud to himself. 'The water's got a golden glow to it.'

Chapter 19

'No… you can't… you mustn't…'

'But we have to Denise… look at him. He's in a very bad way and we can't give him the care he needs here. We have to take him to hospital,' said the older of the two paramedics. They had been called by Brian, the tractor driver. He realised that John needed more help than Denise could give him.

'But you don't understand. He can't leave here… well, he can… but for only a short while.'

'Well, that's OK Denise, with any luck he'll be in and out in no time. The sooner we get him to the hospital, the sooner he'll be back.' She knew the paramedic was right but what if John had to stay for a few days, or even longer? They had spoken many times about the water from under the Yew tree and the water from the pump, and how it kept John young and healthy, and herself now after she had been drinking it… but that was all gone now. What was going to happen? The more she thought about it the more she felt the hospital was the best place for whatever was going to happen, to happen. Then she realised the same would happen to Jack… but he would have to wait. Her main concern right now was John.

'Ok… but I'm coming with you,' she said sternly, moving away from the bed to allow the paramedics to lift John off and into a wheelchair.

'We had to climb over a rickety old bridge in the corner of the field to get here,' said the second paramedic. 'Is there another way back onto the lane out front?'

'Oh… yes… of course. We'll use the front gates. Follow me,' replied Denise dashing to the front door and opening it wide enough for the wheelchair to get through. It had a habit of trying to close itself so she held it open with an outstretched arm as they lifted the chair over the exceptionally high doorstep.

'You stay here Jack… I won't be long… hopefully,' she said looking at Jack who was standing at the kitchen door watching them take his best pal away. He had been with John for over seventy years and although he wasn't showing any emotion… inside he was a mess. John had just saved his life and now he was really ill.

'Don't worry.' He replied quietly. 'Just get him back here… as soon as you can.'

'I will.' Said Denise gently closing the front door.

'Wow,' exclaimed the younger of the two paramedics. 'You and your dog are so close it's as if you talk to each other.' Denise smiled at him as she walked past them to the front gates.

'More than you'll ever know… More than you will ever know.'

She slowly slid the rusty, hard-to-move bolt to one side and swung open the right-hand gate enough for them to get through. The ambulance was parked about twenty yards further along the track where it changed from a half-mud, half-tarmac potholed lane to a fully-fledged muddy farm track, so Denise and one of the paramedics pushed the chair while the other paramedic ran ahead and opened the back doors to the ambulance in readiness for them. The paramedics were well-practised at this sort of thing and within only a few seconds John was out of the wheelchair and laid on a bed with an oxygen mask strapped to his face.

'Not long now Denise,' said the older paramedic who was

staying in the back with them while the younger one did the driving. 'I'm sure he will be all right.'

***

In the hospital, John was wheeled straight into the accident and emergency department and within only a few seconds he was surrounded by doctors and nurses performing all sorts of tests that we mere mortals just have to stand back and watch in awe as these amazing people do what they can to find what's wrong. Denise was asked to stay in the waiting area, which is quite normal in these circumstances as she would only be in the way. She sat as close as possible to the doorway into the triage room so she could react immediately if she was called. Luckily, it was the middle of the afternoon so there were not many people waiting to be attended to, which was a good thing she thought, trying to fill her mind with positive thoughts.

It wasn't long before a nurse came out to speak to her.

'Err... excuse me are you with the gentleman that was brought in by the paramedics?' Denise leapt to her feet pushing the chair hard against the back wall with the backs of her legs.

'Sorry,' she blurted out quickly. 'Yes... Yes... I'm with John.'

'John... That's his name... good. Well...' The nurse paused and instantly Denise's stomach sank making her feel sick.

'What's wrong... is he Ok?'

'Well...' began the nurse again. 'He's in a coma but all his vital signs are perfectly normal and there are no signs of any trauma... anywhere. I was hoping you could tell me what happened?'

Denise stood within arm's length of the nurse and as soon as she asked what had happened a million thoughts swirled around inside her head... how on earth could she describe to the nurse what John had just done... she couldn't tell her he brought his seventy-one-year-old dog back to life by wrapping his arms around him and a massive beam of light had surged through his body. She began to feel light-headed and a little unsteady on her feet so she plonked back down on the hard and unforgiving hospital chair.

'Are you all right?' Asked the nurse putting her hand on Denise's shoulder, 'Would you like a glass of water?'

'Err... Yes please.'

'Ok... I'll only be a minute?' Said the nurse as she turned and walked over to a water dispenser in the corner of the waiting room.

There was a large flat-screen TV mounted on the wall opposite where Denise was sitting. It was there to help pass the time for people waiting for news of their friends and loved ones and was permanently on the news channel. She hadn't paid any attention to it in all the time she had been there but for some reason, her eye was drawn to it just as the nurse returned with her water. It was a NEWSFLASH of something that happened a few hours ago in a small village just outside York... an explosion. Someone had caught everything that had happened above the field on camera as they were walking their dog past John's house. They were unable to record the people in the field because of all the high trees and bushes around the edge but they caught everything else. Denise stood up and walked over to the TV, ignoring the nurse who was trying to hand her the water. After a couple of seconds, Denise turned to the nurse and pointed at the TV.

'That... that's what happened... to John,' she said quietly, obviously in shock.

'John was in an explosion?' Asked the nurse.

'Yes… that one,' said Denise pointing to the TV. The news channel played the ten-second clip of the explosion over and over again because it was like nothing anyone had witnessed before and all the people in the waiting room that were watching were completely awe-struck and not a little bit gobsmacked… even the news presenter said it resembled something from a science fiction film… almost like a biblical event.

'Well that would explain his condition,' said the nurse turning her gaze from the TV and looking at Denise. 'If he's suffered a trauma such as that, his body will be in shock.'

'How long will he be in the coma?' Asked Denise fully aware that John needed to drink the water from under the Yew tree to survive… which was now no longer there.

'That's completely unknown I'm afraid. It could be hours, days or even weeks. It's now up to him.'

'But… but… he can't stay here that long… he has to get home… he just has to.'

'I'm afraid he won't be going anywhere for a while,' said the nurse touching Denise's arm gently and turning to walk back into the room where John was being cared for. She stopped and turned just before walking into the cubicle.

'You sit down and I'll be out again soon to let you know what's happening.'

'Thank you,' replied Denise quietly as she flopped back down into the chair.

Chapter 20

Jack was now on his own at the house and was becoming quite a celebrity amongst the other animals. The word had gotten around that John had brought Jack back from the dead after being hurt under the falling Yew tree, and they wanted to see for themselves how Jack was recovering. Every so often an animal of one type or another would approach Jack and ask for his story, which Jack was more than happy to relate, and as is with many stories such as these, the truth and what actually happened stretched further and further apart... not that Jack was lying, but he loved the attention and just... well... embellished the facts a little, such as how he single-handed, fought off the hundreds of attacking workmen before being crushed by the falling tree... which we all know is almost right... sort of.

It didn't take long for the questions to change from asking about Jack, to where had John and Denise disappeared to... then it hit home for Jack... John had saved his life by what seemed like a miracle... how?

The mood also changed amongst the animals that were arriving at Beckside when they learned of John's amazing intervention with Jack and that now he was ill, which seemed to filter back out into the surrounding fields like a Mexican wave... or an Appleton Roebuck wave to be more accurate. The whole area was bustling with animals and birds chattering, even the bees seemed more active, buzzing around, passing on information to other bee colonies... quite unusual. And the people using the track alongside Beckside, which could number quite a few every day when the weather was good, were aware of something strange happening… a feeling that was hard to explain.

When Denise had left Beckside with John and the paramedics, she had been in such a hurry she had forgotten to close and lock the gates. Jack had done his best to close them but he is only small and the best he could do was push them shut. He obviously was unable to lock them… given his diminutive size.

Now… normally this wouldn't really be a problem, but because the miraculous event with John and Jack had been seen and recorded on a passer-by's phone and shown on the news, just about everyone in the country had seen the explosion of light. Only the people that were in the field at the time knew why it had happened… or… who had caused it, so curious people and journalists were now on the prowl… and the gates to Beckside were unlocked.

***

'Excuse me.' Came a call from the front of the house as Jack was dozing in the back garden on the patio. 'Hello… is anyone here?' Immediately Jack sprung to his feet and ran as fast as his little legs would allow around the outside of the house to the front where he almost bumped into a woman walking in his direction. He skidded to a halt with pieces of gravel flying everywhere as the woman let out a stifled cry and froze to the spot.

'Eeehh,' Jack bared his teeth and growled at her.

'Now then little one,' she said timidly trying to relax and slowly offering him the back of her hand to sniff… which he did. 'Where's the person who lives here?' She said half talking to

Jack, half saying it loud enough that if the owner was in earshot, he or she would show themselves.

'He's not here, and Denise has taken him to the hospital,' said Jack knowing fine well she couldn't hear or understand him. The woman could tell that Jack's bark was worse than his bite and he wasn't going to attack her so she cautiously made her way into the field.

'So... this is where it happened,' she said out loud. She could see the Yew tree had been knocked down and all the bushes and trees around the edge were bent over double, obviously blown down by some large external force... like an explosion. She was a journalist from the local paper and had seen the report on TV. The moment she saw the footage she knew where it had happened as she lived in the next village and had been for a walk many times down the lane... or track, whatever you liked to call it. She had often walked past John's house and had always wondered what it was like on the other side of the tall fences. To her, it reminded her of the secret garden and that was like a red rag to a bull for a journalist. So given a chance to explore... here she was.

She was no explosives expert, but even to her somewhat biased journalistic eyes, it was obvious that it wasn't a typical blast because there was no collateral damage to the house, no huge crater where the blast happened, and no burnt or burning items anywhere.

It was very strange.

It was as if something in the centre created a pressure wave that flattened the trees and the bushes... without actually exploding. Jack had been stood behind her barking for a while but soon gave up when he realised it was pointless because no one was around to hear, so he thought his best course of action was to just follow her… that way if she got up to any mischief he could see what she was doing and report back to John and Denise when they returned… whenever that would be.

She wandered around the field making notes, with Jack a few paces behind watching her every move. She even went as far as the ditch on the far side and was amazed to see the network of waterwheels being used to generate electricity… now that was perfect for the story. Then she made her way to the centre where the Yew tree and the pond were. She could see the tracks from the tractor which came from the bridge in the corner of the field and a huge gouge mark in the bark of the Yew tree indicating where the tractor must have pushed the tree over. She paid little attention to what was left of the pond as she followed the tractor tracks and discovered dozens and dozens of dead crows and other birds.

'What on earth happened here?' She said to herself in disbelief at the sheer number of dead birds.

Again very strange.

'Did you see what happened?' She said turning to look at Jack who just stood there motionless. 'If only you could talk.' She said smiling at him. She turned and wandered back to the Yew tree, where this time she stopped at what used to be the pond and saw the small pool of shimmering golden water.

'Now that's unusual.' She said bending down to take a closer look at the water. Then she caught a glimpse of the water pipe that was almost completely buried under the soil and grass that had accumulated over the years. She crawled along on her hands and knees and fumbling around in the grass, managed to follow it back to the hand pump on the patio where she pumped the handle and watched as the honey-coloured water squirted into the bucket below, She cupped a hand under the water and took a taste.

'Wow.' She said sounding surprised. 'No wonder they've put the pump here... that water tastes brilliant.'

Now her journalistic feelings were bubbling to the surface and she just had to find out who lived here. There was only one thing for it... she would have to have a look inside. The back doors to the sun room and then the kitchen were wide open, as they normally were, so, looking around her to make sure nobody was watching, she made her way inside where everything looked pretty much the same as any other house, except for one thing... well three really. There wasn't a single TV in the place, or radio... and third, the most amazing for today, no phone... of any kind, not even any chargers. These people were cut off from the real world... what kind of people were they? Jack had been following her every move and was now standing behind her as she opened the drawers one by one to the hallway table which had four drawers. In the last drawer, she found what she was looking for... a letter, a very old letter with a name... John Ryder... dated 1953. She took a deep breath and slowly opened it trying not to damage the old and slightly crumbling envelope. The paper of the letter was a faded yellow colour and it was a letter from John Ryder's solicitors congratulating him on the purchase of Beckside... this house.

Now she had a name and a date she could leave, happy in the knowledge that she could do some research to find out more about the people that lived in this rather strange but wonderful house.

Chapter 21

There was a knock on the door and then a squeak and a whoosh as the door to the room was slowly pushed open.

'Hello. Do you mind if I come in?'

Denise looked up from the bedside chair and shook her head meaning she didn't mind. Over the last twenty-four hours or so, so many different people had come and gone that another made no difference. They had been visited by umpteen doctors still trying to understand why John was in the condition he was, and nurses came, what seemed like every few minutes to monitor his vital signs, blood pressure, temperature etc.

'I'm so sorry to bother you. My name's Carol... Carol Parker from the local newspaper. Do you mind if I ask you some questions?' She said trying to keep her voice down. Denise looked up from the chair and scowled at her.

'What about? Who let you in here?'

'I won't be long. I know it's not easy but I just wanted to talk to you about the explosion,' said Carol almost whispering.

Denise was tired and confusion swept across her mind... then it registered. What happened at Beckside was seen on TV and to everyone who wasn't there, the lights and the hurricane-like winds seemed like an explosion.

'Oh... err... Ok,' she replied looking at John lying calmly in the hospital bed. Carol pulled up another chair that was against the wall and put it at the end of the bed where she sat down. She put her bag on the floor and pulled out a pad and a pen which she put on her lap, followed by her mobile phone.

'You don't mind if I record this do you?'

'Err... no... whatever.'

'So... just for the record... you are?'

'Denise... Denise Williamson.'

'And John Ryder is here... in the bed,' said Carol pointing at John.

'Yes,' replied Denise quietly.

'So... Can you tell me exactly what happened in the field at Beckside Denise?'

Now... Denise may have been a little tired and confused but she knew that telling anyone who hadn't witnessed what had happened first-hand would be difficult for them to understand.

'Yes. John was in an explosion in the field... and now he's here... in a coma.'

'What was he doing Denise... why was there an explosion?'

'He was working in the field, cutting the grass, bushes... and stuff, when a storm came and then there was an explosion... and here he is,' she said pointing to John and hoping that her explanation sounded convincing enough.

'Why was there an explosion Denise... was there a lightning strike or something?'

Relieved that Carol had suggested a lightning strike, she went along with it.

'Yes... there must have been.'

'But I went to the field Denise and there were no signs of a lightning strike. No burn marks. Nothing. What really happened?' Denise had been looking at John the whole time but now turned to glare at Carol, knowing she had been deceived.

'You've been to Beckside?' She growled through her clenched teeth.

'Yes. I had seen the explosion on the TV and went to see what had happened. To try and talk to someone to get some answers.'

'How did you get in?'

'The gates were unlocked... so I went in, but there was no one there... you're here. Although I see there are only two of you... Where is Mr Ryder's elderly father?'

'His father... what do you mean?'

'Well... I presume this is the young Mr Ryder... I just thought... Oh... I'm sorry. He has passed away... my mistake.'

'What on earth are you talking about?' Said Denise raising her voice slightly as she was now getting to the point where she had had enough of questions. 'Look I think it's time you were leaving. John needs to rest.'

Carol stood up frustrated at not getting the answers she wanted and started to put everything back in her bag when Denise caught a glimpse of John's letter. She immediately grabbed it.

'What's this?' She said waving it around. 'This is addressed to John. How did you get it?' Carol had to think quickly.

'It was on the table in the hallway and I picked it up by mistake.'

'You were in the house?'

'Yes... I'm sorry... I was just looking for the owner or owners so I could talk to them about the explosion. You have a lovely dog.'

'Jack was there?'

'If Jack is your dog... then yes... he followed me around everywhere,' Denise felt slightly better knowing Jack had seen her and followed her around... at least when she saw him again he would be able to tell her exactly what happened... talking to the animals has its advantages.

Carol handed Denise her business card.

'Here's my card. If there's anything you want to tell me please give me a call... or a text... or email.' She said with a smile on her face. 'Oh... do you mind if I can have a picture of you two?' But before Denise could answer, there was a flash of light from Carol's phone and the picture had been taken. 'Thank you.'

'Ok... Goodbye,' said Denise glad to see the back of her as she left the room. Everything could now return to being quiet and peaceful.

***

Carol got into her car which was parked in the hospital's high-rise carpark and threw her bag onto the passenger seat. Then... something made her get her phone out of her bag and check the picture she had just taken of John and Denise. It looked like a perfectly normal picture of someone in a hospital bed, apart from there seemed to be a ring of light around John's head and shoulders. It looked very strange. It had never happened before and it meant that she now had to get another picture because she couldn't use this one for the newspaper piece.

'Ohh....Damn,' she exclaimed throwing her phone into her bag.

'Damn... Damn... Damn...'

Exceedingly annoyed and frustrated at herself for not checking the picture while she was with Denise, She grabbed her bag and returned to John's room. She knocked on the door and slowly pushed it open half expecting Denise to shout at her but fortunately, the room was empty apart from John lying peacefully in the bed.

She stood at the end of his bed looking carefully at how he was laid, the light coming from the window and the strip lights on the ceiling but there was nothing obviously wrong so she raised her phone and took a picture. Before taking another she previewed the picture… but there was still a ring of light around his head and shoulders… was the lens dirty? She wiped it and took another shot… still the same.

'I need to take a picture of someone else to make sure the phone's working all right,' she mumbled to herself just as a nurse came in.

'Oh… Hi,' said Carol a little shocked at her sudden appearance. 'Do you mind if I take a picture of you with John?'

'Does Denise know you're here?' Asked the young female nurse guardedly.

'Yes… Yes of course. I'm just waiting for her to get back… she's gone for a coffee,' said Carol hoping Denise hadn't told anyone where she had gone. Years of working as a journalist had taught her to think and react quickly.

'Oh… well. OK then… how do you want me?'

'If you could just stand over John as if you were attending to him.' The nurse stood at the edge of the bed as requested. 'That's excellent.' Said Carol as she took a couple of pictures from slightly different angles. 'Thank you.'

'You're welcome,' replied the nurse with a smile as she checked John was OK and left the room. Carol scrolled through her phone and checked the pictures she had just taken but they were the same… there was still a hazy white light around John but not the nurse. As she studied the photos Denise came into the room.

'HEY,' Denise cried, walking quickly over to the bed and running her hands over John to make sure he was Ok. 'What the hell do you think you're doing?'

Carol took a step back and unusually for a journalist, owned up.

'Denise... I'm really sorry....'

'You'd better get out,' said Denise sternly, not letting Carol finish her sentence and gesturing with her arm towards the door.

'Hear me out Denise... Something very strange is going on here.'

'What... What do you mean?' Said Denise defensively.

'Well... Well... There's no easy way to tell you... I'll just show you,' So Carol showed Denise the last few pictures she had just taken of John alone and the ones with the nurse. 'What do you think?'

'Your camera must be faulty?'

'No... No... Look,' replied Carol as she took another quick shot of Denise by the bed with John, immediately looking at the picture and showing it to Denise...it was the same...a hazy white-light effect around John and nothing around Denise. Denise had not seen this before but she instantly knew it was something to do with the water from the pond and the Yew tree. She walked over to the chair and plonked herself down putting her hands in her lap and drooping her head forward.

'What is it Denise? Are you Ok?' She didn't answer for a couple of seconds and then looked straight at Carol. 'You know something don't you... you have to tell me Denise.'

'No... I can't.'

'Come on Denise... Maybe I can help?'

'No... How?... How can you help me Carol?'

'I don't know... but please,' said Carol kneeling in front of Denise and looking her in the eye. 'I know I come across as an in-your-face journalist but I am here to help you... Do you need to get some clothes… or anything… for John…? I could give you a lift home and back again.' Denise was starting to feel more scared for John than she had been at any time and she didn't have anyone to talk to… Maybe Carol could help?

'Look…' began Denise. 'If I tell you what I know… will you help us… John and I?'

'Yes… yes of course… if I can help…I will.'

'Ok,' said Denise standing up and moving over to sit on the bed with John. 'Sit down in the chair and I'll tell you everything… believe me… you'll need to sit down.'

'Brilliant… thank you,' said Carol sitting down and switching her phone on to record the audio while resting it on her lap.

'Ok… I suppose the best place to start is at the beginning… so here goes.' Said Denise taking a breath.

Denise spent the next thirty minutes or so telling Carol everything that had happened to her over the last few months and everything John had told her… about his life and the time he'd spent at Beckside while Carol recorded everything, occasionally making notes in her notebook.

'So… And that's how John got to be here… in the hospital bed… what do you think?' Carol just stared at her for a few seconds with a rather blank look on her face, until finally she answered.

'What do I think….well… it's a very nice story… but come on Denise… you're pulling my leg? Humans can't talk to animals… and the other way around. John can't make clouds begin to appear… or bring his dog back to life… with a beam of light.'

'I knew you wouldn't believe me,' said Denise sliding off the bed and standing to look out of the window.

'The clouds were probably a storm... with lightning or something... that's all.'

'Ok... Ok... I told you I would tell you everything... I can't make you believe me... so now what Carol?' She turned to look at Carol who was leaning against the bed looking in her direction when she noticed John twitch.

'Oh my God... John just moved,' she said rushing to his side and grabbing his hand. 'He moved... he did... he just moved Carol.'

'He's still asleep Denise... look at him... It was probably just a twitch... but look,' she showed Denise the picture of him from a couple of hours ago and now. 'Does he look different to you?' They both studied the picture and then John's face... first the picture... then John... back and forward many times. Denise started to cry.

'Oh no Carol... it's started.'

'What? What's started?'

'What I told you about him drinking the water. He hasn't had any for far too long... he's starting to age.'

'No... surely...'

'I'm telling you Carol. It's started. If I don't get him some water from home... well... god only knows.'

'Ok... come on Denise my car's in the car park. If we go now we can be back within two hours...' she said trying to pull Denise away from the bed.

'I'll be back as soon as I can,' Said Denise trying to kiss John on his forehead as she was being dragged away.

Chapter 22

The traffic was bad as usual as they sped their way back to Beckside, but it wasn't long before they were bouncing around in the car navigating through the minefield of potholes on the dusty track leading to the house. Carol hit the brakes hard causing her car to skid to a halt by the bridge, narrowly missing the white railings that were there to stop anyone falling into the ditch.

'Sorry… that was a bit close.' She exclaimed as they both leapt out and ran to the gates which Jack had pushed together as best he could. Throwing the left-hand gate to one side, they both ran down the drive and round the back where Jack was waiting for them… along with dozens of other animals ranging from the biggest dear to the smallest mouse.

'The Kestrel told me you were coming,' said Jack as they both stopped in their tracks on the patio by the doors to the sunroom.

'We need to get some water for John… he… he…' Denise tried to get the words out but she needn't have bothered because Jack knew exactly why.

'He's getting old.'

'Yes… you knew?' She said sounding surprised.

'Hey… I may be old but I'm not stupid. We both need the water… right.'

'Are you talking to that dog?' Asked Carol, looking at them both with her head cocked to one side like a confused Labrador.

'Oh… Yes… Jack… Carol… Carol… Jack.'

'Err... Hello Jack... we've met before haven't we.'

'Yes,' replied Jack looking straight at her. 'This is the woman that came into the house and went through John's stuff.'

'I know... I know... we'll talk about it later,' said Denise as she walked over to the garage and opened the door.

'What's he saying Denise?' Asked Carol a little nervous as to what Jack had said.

'He said... you're the woman that came to the house and went through our stuff.'

'Well... I...' spluttered Carol.

'Forget it Carol... I'm trying to find....ah got it,' she said almost sprinting out of the garage to the water pump while carrying a white plastic water container that could hold about a gallon of water. 'This should do for now.' Carol stood next to the pump and began to pump the lever up and down.

'I'm not going to use that water... I know it comes from the field but I want to make sure it's as pure as it can be... come on... let's get this thing filled up.' They ran into the field towards the toppled Yew tree with the animals following their every step and surrounding them as Denise put the water container into the water and it slowly began to fill.

'This is quite intimidating,' said Carol looking around at the dozens of animals encircling them.

'What the...' cried Denise in amazement.

'I know... it began growing yesterday and it hasn't stopped.' Said Jack sniffing the stem of the new Yew tree sapling.

'How has it grown so quickly?... It's a Yew Tree... They grow really slowly,' exclaimed Carol flapping her arms around in dismay. 'It must be five feet tall... that's not possible... when I was here the other day there wasn't even a shoot... nothing.'

'You see... It's like everything that happens here Carol...

this place is special... that's why we need to preserve it... and stop them building houses here.'

'Yes... Yes..." You're right," she stuttered still trying to get her head around what was happening at Beckside.

"There... it's full... come on Carol... let's get back to the hospital and give this to John.'

'Yes... Yes of course,' Carol replied still in a daze as they both ran away from the Yew tree and across the field, watching the animals scramble out of the way to avoid being stood on or bumped into.

'Look after the place Jack... I don't know when I'll be back,' cried Denise without even looking back.

'Don't worry... Just get John back here as soon as you can.' Jack shouted back.

'I still find it hard to believe and completely bizarre that you can talk to the animals... and they answer back,' said Carol panting out of breath as they got to the gates of the house.

'I know... It took me a while to get used to it as well... but I wouldn't change it for the world now... come on... let's get in the car and back to the hospital ASAP.'

***

It had only taken about twenty minutes to get the water and within another half an hour or so they were pulling into the car park back at the hospital. Five minutes later they were stood in John's hospital room completely out of breath and armed with a gallon of golden nectar.

'What's wrong?' Panted Denise almost dropping the water container on the floor as she bundled her way through a group of nurses and doctors standing around John's bed. 'What's going on?' Although as soon as she'd got those words out of her mouth it was blatantly obvious what was wrong. 'Oh no... John... John.' She leaned forward slightly and took hold of his hand with hers... it was cold and clammy.

'Denise... what is it? Asked Carol pushing her way to the front of the medical staff standing around the bed and then raising her hand to cover her mouth in shock. 'Oh my God.'

John had begun to age at an alarming rate while they had been away and he was now almost unrecognisable... he looked so old... because he was old.

'The nurse came in to check on Mr Ryder and saw his condition,' said one of the doctors. 'I... We... We have never witnessed anything like this before. It's as if he is ageing one year for every minute... it's... it's incredible. We don't know what to do.'

'I do,' said Denise turning round and shoving them all out of the way as she lunged behind her for the water container. She then grabbed a plastic cup from beside his bed and filled it with the golden water... although the water had lost its golden colour and was now more of an insipid yellow.

'What's that?' Said one of the doctors loudly, concerned as to what she was giving John.

'It's water,' replied Denise hurriedly as she poured the water into the cup splashing some over the bed by mistake. 'Special water.'

'It doesn't look like something you should be giving him'

'Trust me... it is... special water for a special human being,' Denise put her hand under the back of John's head and tilted him forward slightly to allow the water from the cup to enter his mouth... hopefully without choking him. He swallowed. She let some more trickle into his mouth and then let him swallow again.

She did this a few times until the cup was empty.

'Is that enough?' Whispered Carol.

'I don't know...' Denise replied letting his head fall gently back onto the pillow.

'How long do we wait?' Whispered Carol again.

'Carol,' said Denise raising her voice in frustration at being asked questions she didn't know the answer to. 'I don't know... all right?'

'Sorry.

They waited... and waited... and waited... and after about twenty minutes, the doctors and nurses shuffled out of the room mumbling and talking amongst themselves leaving Denise and Carol with John. The last nurse to leave the room turned and smiled at them as she pulled the door to.

'Let us know if his condition changes,' she said clicking the door shut.

Denise had not moved from John's bedside and was holding his hand with both of hers. She leaned forward and softly whispered in his ear.

'John. If you can hear me. Come back... come back to me... I don't know what to do.' Tears formed in her eyes which welled up and overflowed like a stream breaking its banks cascading down her face as she kissed him on his forehead and then his nose. As she pulled back slightly to look at him she could see her tears on his cheeks.

'Oh... look at me,' she whispered and smiled as she gently wiped them away from his face. 'I'm leaking all over you.'

After another hour or so of patiently waiting and constantly monitoring John's condition, Denise was becoming more and more agitated, pacing up and down in the small room, sitting on the bed, in the chair, on the window ledge. Finally, Carol, who had been sitting quietly in one of the hard-backed chairs felt she had to say something.

'Denise. Please. I know it's difficult for you… but we have to give it time.'

Denise spun round from where she had been looking out of the window.

'Carol,' she said firmly looking straight at her. 'The one thing we don't have is time. The longer we wait… the older John gets.' She walked over to his bed and suddenly gasped, raising her hands to her mouth as if to stifle a scream. Carol instantly looked up from her notepad.

'What is it?'

'Oh… No… No,' she said almost falling onto the bed in shock.

'What… What?' Carol said quickly moving over to have a look at John. 'Oh… Now what do we do?'

Denise barged Carol out of the way as she grabbed the water container she'd brought from Beckside, which was now on the floor next to the bed. She snatched the plastic cup from the bedside cabinet and filled it with water again but it was obvious something wasn't right.

'Look.' She said thrusting the cup into Carol's face. 'Look at it.'

'What… What am I looking at?' Carol said moving the cup back slightly into her range of focus. 'I can't see….'

'Look at it Carol… look closely,' Carol swirled the water around and around in the cup but she couldn't see anything wrong and as she looked at Denise with a confused look on her face, Denise plonked herself down on the hard-backed chair Carol had been sitting in.

'It's clear Carol.'

'Yes… Oh…' said Carol suddenly realising what Denise meant.

'Oh… Yes… it should be yellow, a golden yellow. The water's not going to work Carol… it's not going to work,' she leant forward in the chair, putting her hands up to cover her face as Carol walked over to her and knelt to give her a huge hug.

'I don't know what to say Denise…'

After a few moments of quietly hugging each other, Denise stood up almost kneeing Carol in the face.

'There's only one thing we can do,' Denise said sternly, looking blankly at the wall opposite. 'We have to get John back to Beckside… right away… immediately.'

Carol pulled herself up off the floor using the bed to lean on.

'Err… Ok… I've never done this before. Do we just walk out… what do we do?' Denise turned and stood so close to Carol that their noses almost touched.

'Yep… That's what we're going to do… and if they won't let me take him, then you're going to distract them while I get him out of here.'

Chapter 23

It wasn't long after Denise and Carol had left Beckside that a few animals began to congregate in the field around the rapidly growing new Yew tree sapling, and some were even wandering into the house to talk with Jack who was in his bed at the bottom of the stairs. He didn't mind. They were only concerned for John's well-being and wanted a bit more information as to how John was. The trouble was... Jack didn't know any more than they did, so rather than tell them anything, he just said that John was getting better and would be back soon. The problem with this was that animals are extremely resourceful creatures and unbeknown to Jack, the word had got back to one or two of the animals that John was in a serious way and may not survive.

Jack decided to go into the field to try and talk to all the animals as a group, that way he felt he would be able to set their minds at ease and stop them worrying because John had helped them and their families so many times over the years, they all felt as if John was one of them... one of the animals. As Jack wandered towards the small pond next to the new Yew tree, which had already magically grown to look like a small tree after only a couple of days, one of the rabbits called out that he'd heard John was ill and might not make it back.

'How do you know that?' Said Jack angrily showing his teeth.

'Sorry Jack... but some of the birds here have been talking to other birds from the city. They have been outside the hospital and heard humans talking about John... getting really old... really quickly... and the humans don't know what to do.'

Jack knew this was probably true and apologised to the rabbit.

'I'm sorry for snarling at you... but like everyone here... I'm worried for John too.'

'What can we do for him?' Came a cry from a squirrel clinging to one of the branches in the Yew tree.

'We must be able to do something.' Asked one of the foxes sitting next to the small pool of water where the pond was originally.

'Look....' called out Jack trying to calm everyone down. 'All we can do is hope he gets better.' Then... out of the silence came a voice... a very small, quiet voice.

'What if we do what other humans do and pray to their God?'

Jack looked around at all the animals trying to identify the speaker... and right at the back of the crowd, about ten feet away was a mouse standing on the back of large male deer.

'We don't pray to a God do we,' replied Jack quietly. '... and neither did John.'

'Err... Excuse me,' said the mouse politely. 'But I don't think that's exactly right. My father always told my brothers and sisters how John healed his broken back. He couldn't do it at first, but he prayed to the energy in the Yew tree and the golden pond... and the miracle happened... he healed my father.'

You could have heard a baby Robin tweet it was so quiet at that moment. Jack sat down on the grass with a plonk.

'Your father... was his name Fus?' He asked.

'Yes.'

'I remember it well... and your father was right.'

'So... if John could pray to the energy in the tree and the

water… why can't we?'

The animals began to talk and chatter amongst themselves as Jack slowly stood up.

'I think,' Jack said, as instantly the animals went quiet in anticipation. 'I think… it would be good if we did the same… who knows my friends… it might just work.'

With their newfound hope, they all crowded around the new Yew tree and the pool of water becoming a pond again and began to hold a silent vigil, all praying in their own little way to whatever energy it was in the tree and the water that helped John heal the mouse… and all the other creatures. Some of the crows began talking and decided it would be good to get some more birds and animals together… maybe, they thought, the more of them that prayed, the more chance they could heal… or at least help John, so they flew off in every direction in the hope of persuading other animals to help in their quest to save John.

Chapter 24

'They're not going to let us just walk out of here with him... he has to sign himself out and he can't... he's asleep,' said Denise stating the obvious, although she wasn't really talking to Carol, just making a point. 'He can't walk so we need a wheelchair... Carol... go see if you can find a wheelchair. I think there are some by the main entrance if you can't find one around here.'

'Ok, 'replied Carol hesitantly. 'But won't they stop me?'

'I've no idea... but if they do... lie... you're a journalist... you must be good at lying,' said Denise shrugging her shoulders and smiling at Carol who was beginning to wish she had never met Denise.

Carol opened the door and slowly popped her head out into the corridor checking in both directions before walking out confidently, hoping that if she had been seen, no one was paying attention or cared what she was doing. The door closed with a whooshing sound behind her.

Denise had found John's clothes in the cupboard next to his bed and was busy dressing him. She felt a little embarrassed because although they had shared a house for a while now, they had never been intimate... and well... how much more intimate could she get than what she was doing right now... apart from having sex.

'Stop it,' she said to herself as she threw his covers back. 'Just get him dressed and then we're out of here.'

After about five minutes of struggling and manipulating

John's limp body, she finally managed to get his clothes on and stood back from the bed to admire her handy work. 'Phew.' She said wiping her brow. 'That was hard work. I'm glad I don't have to do that every day.' The thought of her and John being intimate had completely left her mind as she was now completely focused on getting him out of the hospital and back home.

While she was waiting for Carol to return she stood by the side of the bed studying John's face and she realised, in all the time she had known him, she had never done that before. It then crossed her mind that how many people actually did that… studied someone's face… all their imperfections, wrinkles, moles… how one eye was slightly lower than the other, how long the hairs were on their eyebrows, what size and shape their ears were, how big their nose was… the hairs growing out of their nose… so many things that we all just take for granted and never really notice, or at least, not until something really serious happens… and then it's almost too late. A smile slowly crept across her face and her head tilted to one side as she stretched out her arm to touch his cheek with the palm of her hand. The second she made contact with his skin, whether it was coincidence or the touch of her skin on his, he gave a shudder from head to foot and seemed to instantly age a few more years. She recoiled her hand back in horror… had she just caused that to happen? She ran to the door and yanked it open looking first one way down the corridor and then the other… but Carol was nowhere to be seen. Just as she was about to back into the room, the buzzer on the elevator down the corridor sounded and out strolled Carol wheeling a sturdy maroon-coloured wheelchair in front of her. Denise kept the door to the room open with one arm and frantically waved her along with her other arm hoping it would make Carol speed up a little… but Carol kept her calm to not create attention and manoeuvred the wheelchair into the room at a normal walking pace.

'Quick... will you please hurry up,' said Denise sounding panicky.

'I came as quickly as I could Denise... I've only been gone a few minutes... what's the matter?'

'John is ageing more rapidly... we need to get out of here as quickly as we can. I've dressed him so all we need to do now is lift him into the chair.'

Which was easier said than done. If you've ever tried to lift a limp, flexible, unevenly shaped dead weight then you will know how difficult it is... and after a couple of failed attempts to gently lift him off the bed, they decided the best way was to let gravity do most of the work by pushing, guiding and finally dropping him into the chair with a thump. It wasn't very dignified... but it worked.

'That was harder than I thought it was going to be.' Panted Carol almost out of breath. Denise stood and looked at him for a second realising he looked very conspicuous in the chair.

'We need to cover him with something otherwise they'll recognise him... what about his white blanket from the bed?' She said reaching behind her and dragging it off the bed.

'Good idea. Put his hands on his lap and drape it over his legs.' Instructed Carol as if she had done this before. 'What about his face? They will see him and recognise him immediately.'

'You're right,' exclaimed Denise looking around her. There was a waist-high shelving rack next to the bed with plastic containers full of various medical items so she quickly pulled them out one at a time and rummaged around for something she could use.

'This'll do,' she said excitedly pulling out a small white face mask, the type the doctors and nurses use. She ripped open the plastic bag and slid it over John's face to cover his nose and mouth. 'Perfect.'

'What about his hair Denise... won't they recognise him from his hair?'

'Too late to do anything about that Carol... we need to get out of here... now,' said Denise grabbing the handles of the wheelchair and shoving him towards the door which Carol had already begun to open.

'You go first... is it all clear?'

Carol looked up and down the corridor and apart from the occasional nurse wandering about doing their normal everyday tasks, it was all clear.

'Yes... let's go.'

The pair of them moved as quickly as they dare towards the elevators.

'Carol... press the button to go down... quickly.'

Luckily as soon as she pressed the button the door opened... and it was empty. Carol entered first, getting ready to push the button for the ground floor as soon as they were in place.

'Go,' said Denise slightly out of breath. The doors closed and it seemed to take an eternity to reach the ground floor... but in reality was probably only twenty seconds or so. The doors opened with a ping and they were confronted with dozens of sick, injured and generally confused people milling around in the lobby of the hospital. They pushed their way through and headed for the main entrance which was a good fifty yards or so away... you forget just how big hospitals are. They were walking quite quickly considering they were pushing someone in a wheelchair, but fortunately, no one noticed...or at least, didn't say anything, so they were incredibly relieved to reach the main doors where they stopped and smiled at each other.

'We've done it,' whispered Carol thankful they had managed to get as far as they had.

'I'll believe we've made it when we get back to Beckside,' replied Denise pushing the wheelchair and John towards the large glass automatic doors which slid open with a shushing sound. All in all, there were three sets of sliding doors to get through before getting outside… designed to keep as much heat in the huge building as possible in times of extreme cold, which today wasn't one of them. It was a gloriously sunny and warm day outside.

As they sauntered along the path to the car park glad to be free of the sanitized air of the hospital, they could hear a commotion behind them. It was one of the nurses who had treated John. She had recognised them and was shouting and waving her arms in the air. They were too far away but knew whatever she was saying was not good news, so they ran as fast as they could to the multi-storey carpark where Carol's car was parked.

They struggled to get John into the small car and ended up pushing him head-first onto the back seat. They couldn't take the wheelchair so they left it pushed up against one of the supporting concrete pillars, which they didn't like to do, but they were in too much of a hurry to take it back to the lobby… and anyway, they would probably have got caught by security… or the police.

Carol put her foot down as soon as they left the car park heading for the main road and behind them she could see what looked like police running to get into a car… probably to chase them.

'I think we are going to be in a police chase,' said Carol rather calmly for someone who was now a fugitive. Denise turned round to look out the back window and confirmed what Carol had just said.

'Yep... get a move on Carol... they'll be with us in no time if you don't.' Luckily like any major city nowadays, traffic is a terrible problem and today was no different in York. In fact, it was probably as bad as it had been in a long time... all it needed was for one road to be closed in the city and everything ground to a halt. Somehow they managed to lose the police car by using all the back roads and alleyways in the city until they got onto the main road out of York where, again they were stuck in a traffic jam waiting to get onto the ring road, the A64, which led within a few miles of the village and then to Beckside. Once on the A64, it was a short journey to the turn-off for the village which only took about five minutes on the winding B road and when they were about halfway along they noticed a low-flying helicopter in front of them... it was a Police helicopter... they had been spotted.

'Now what do we do?' Asked Carol leaning forward over the steering wheel as much as she dare to look up at the helicopter.

'Keep going Carol... we have to get to Beckside... we're nearly there.'

Within two minutes they were entering the village and approaching the turn-off for the road that leads to Beckside but just as they were turning into the road, a police car came round the forty-five-degree bend in the main street, just a little further along from where they were and spotted them. Immediately the police switched on the blue flashing light with the siren and chased after them swerving to avoid hitting the curb as they turned into Bond Lane.

'We're almost there,' cried Carol... but she said it too soon because when they were only a few yards from the track that led to Beckside another Police car driving from the opposite direction screeched to a halt in front of them blocking their way. Carol almost jumped on the brake pedal spinning the steering wheel around and causing the car to skid sideways to a halt narrowly missing the police blocking their path.

'NOOO....' cried Denise turning in her seat to look behind her at John, who had been thrown forward but luckily they had fastened a seat belt around him and he was Ok. He was leant to one side with his head slumped forward but still in one piece.

The four policemen, two from each car, had jumped out of their cars and were standing around the car screaming at them to get out... slowly.

'We have to get John to his house,' yelled Denise as she opened the back door to the car and one of the policemen tackled her to the floor. 'NOOO...' she cried as he pulled her to her feet and threw her against the car. 'If we don't get John to his house... at the other end of the track... he'll die.'

One of the policemen who was older than the rest leaned into the back of the car and checked on John.

'This man appears to be unconscious and in need of medical attention,' he said turning to look at Denise. 'You removed this man from the hospital and we have been asked to return him... for his own wellbeing.'

'No... you don't understand... I have to get him to his house,' she said shaking herself loose from the policemen's grip and pointing to the house at the end of the lane.

'Why... why to his house... why not back to the hospital?' He replied as he turned to look towards the end of the lane.

'It'll take too long to explain... I just have to,' she pleaded in desperation.

'I grew up around here... is the gentleman in the back of the car Mr Ryder?'

'Yes… Yes… do you know him?'

'Well… No… but I know of him… he's lived there for as long as I can remember… he must be really old by now?'

'Yes… that's why I need to get him to his house… please…'

'Err… excuse me… but have you seen this?' Interrupted one of the other policemen who was looking at something down the track towards John's house. All the policemen including Carol and Denise, took a couple of paces away from the car and shielding their eyes from the sun with their hands, looked in wonder at what was happening.

'What the hell is going on?'

'What is it?'

'Why the…' Said three of the policemen one after another.

'It's the animals,' Denise said softly. 'They've come to meet us.'

'What? The animals?' Said the older policeman. 'Why… how?'

Chapter 25

It was an incredible sight to behold.

The dirt track that led to John's house was approximately a hundred yards long and just wide enough for two average-sized cars. On the left were seven houses set back from the road and on the right was a large ditch about ten feet across with flowing water that varied from a few inches in depth during a dry summer to almost overflowing after a long spell of heavy rain. Beyond the ditch were fields with John's house sandwiched between them. Normally the track was completely free of any cars or obstructions but today was different.

As Denise, Carol and the four policemen stood in awe at what they could see ahead of them, Denise turned to the older of the policemen.

'You see... they have come to greet John on his return. Please. You have to let me take John to his house at the end of the track. If nothing happens when we getthere we can go back to the hospital... but please let me try.'

'I...I... I have lived around here all my life and I have never witnessed anything like this. Ok... Let's go to the house,' he said as bewildered, confused... and amazed as the rest. Denise returned to the car.

'Can someone help me get John out of the car please?' She called from the back seat as she removed his seatbelt and took hold of his arms.

'Oh... where am I?' John mumbled with half-opened eyes.

'Oh my God... you're awake,' said Denise pulling him towards her and giving him a huge hug.

'Wow,' he said sounding surprised. 'What's that for?'

'It's... for... being... awake... and... alive,' she said kissing his face and talking at the same time.

'Are we home?'

'Yes... Yes... come on let's get you out and back to the house.'

John had aged hugely from being away from Beckside and his body had returned to that of a ninety or one-hundred-year-old man. He was slow at moving around, as happens when we get old, and found it difficult to stand upright for any length of time, which meant it wasn't going to be easy walking down the track to the house. The older policeman had come to her call for help and taking John's hands, gently pulled him out of the car where Denise put her arm around his waist on one side and the policeman held his arm on the other. As soon as John caught sight of the sheer number of animals that had come to greet him, he seemed to become more energized and stood more upright, puffing out his chest.

He turned to the policeman smiling.

'Thank you... but I'm all right now.'

'Err... Ok... are you sure?'

'Yes... Thank you,' John said cracking a smile.

The policeman slowly let go of his arm and let him stand on his own with Denise holding his hand. The pair of them began to walk slowly along the track with Carol and the four policemen following a few paces behind.

It was almost impossible to see the ground ahead or the trees and bushes on both sides for the sheer number of birds and creatures of all shapes and sizes perched, sat or stood along the track. It was like a sea of animals that parted as they approached and reformed behind them leaving a small clear circle of space for them to walk in unhindered.

As they made their way along the dusty, potholed track towards the house it was noticeable how quiet it was. Normally you would be able to hear the chatter and song of the birds all around but for some reason, they remained silent... hardly a sound. Every tree, branch, twig, bush and hedge was covered in birds with Swallows, Swifts and House Martins darting back and forth above. Higher in the sky Red Kites and Buzzards could be seen soaring majestically, swooping down to get a closer look and casting huge shadows on John and everyone below.

They had to tread extremely carefully as they walked along because mice, voles, rats and a multitude of other small creatures were zipping around their feet, and the last thing they wanted to do was stand on one.

After a few minutes of walking slowly along the track, they approached the bridge and the gates to the house which were shut, but before they could reach the gates they had to navigate their way through the animals blocking their way. Dancing along the railings to the bridge and along the top of the fence, even the tops of the gates, were dozens of squirrels of all sizes ... who, even when the gates were pushed open, didn't move.

'Oh my God,' whispered Denise in amazement at what she could see waiting for them all.

John insisted on going through the gates unaided and as he slowly walked into Beckside, he stumbled a little on the uneven ground making Denise and Carol behind lunge forward to grab hold of him.

'Are you all right?' Asked Denise.

'Yes... yes... I'm fine.'

'Is he all right?' Asked the older policeman leaning forward to ask Denise.

'Yes he's fine… just a little tired I think.'

'I'm just amazed at all these wonderful creatures that have come to see me,' said John, appearing very frail again.

'We need to get you over to the water in the field… and quickly I think,' said Denise signalling to Carol to help her hold him.

In front of them was an ocean of animals, large and small, tall and short, hairy and furry, making it impossible to count how many. There were birds in every tree and bush, small animals in every conceivable nook and cranny… so many it was difficult to believe there were that many animals around here.

'I'm just gobsmacked… it's unbelievable… there's so many of them,' said one of the younger policemen looking around him in amazement. 'Where have they all come from?'

'Some of these are the animals that John has cared for over the years… see that Badger over there, John healed his broken ankle… and that Deer… there… he healed a wound she had in her side from barbed wire… there are just too many to mention,' whispered Denise.

'Wow… amazing,' gasped the policeman.

'I know… you don't know the half of it. We have to get John into the field as soon as possible.'

'Why into the field… why not indoors?'

'It's a long story… just help us get him into the field.'

'Ok… you two lead the way and I'll be right behind you.'

Denise and Carol supported John as best they could as they made their way slowly along the drive and along the front of the house where Jack was sitting on the front step watching the action.

'Hello you.'

'Hello old friend,' replied John. It was the first time he had seen Jack since the incident in the field. 'How do you feel?'

'I'm good... Thank you for bringing me back from the dead,' said Jack with a doggy smile.

'Aww...' replied John grinning. 'You would have done the same for me.'

'Get into the field... and get some of that water down you old timer,' said Jack giving himself a good shake.

'Ok... go ladies. Get to the water.'

Denise and Carol very gently moved John along the path at the front of the house until it came to the field edge where the policemen behind began talking amongst themselves.

'Was he talking to that dog?'

'It certainly looked like it?'

'How... how can a human talk to a dog?'

'Hey... what about the dog talking to him?'

Denise turned to them with a huge smile on her face.

'One day guys... I'll tell you how it works... but until then let's just get John over to that tree over there... wow Carol... have you seen how big the new Yew tree is now... it's almost full size.'

'Incredible,' Carol replied. 'Although nothing in this place surprises me any more.'

'Haha... I know what you mean,' laughed Denise.

Slowly they made their way through the multitude of earth's creatures assembled as far as the eye could see in the field and beyond, and when they were about five yards away from the Yew tree John stopped and stretched his arms out sideways.

'Stop here please.'

'What… Why… we need to get you to the water.'

'Let go of me please… thank you…I'll get it from here.'

'But… but…'

'No buts… you're not a goat,' he said smiling at Denise. 'I have to get it from here.'

'Ok,' she replied grudgingly. 'But be careful.'

He nodded at her and gently touched the ends of her fingers as he took a small step forward. He stood motionless for a second facing the Yew tree when all of a sudden he fell to his knees.

'NO,' screamed Denise as she lunged towards him but instantly her way was blocked by hundreds of animals and birds swirling and churning around. 'STOP,' she cried again. But it was no good, the animals completely blocked her way not letting her through. She felt a tugging on her jeans and when she looked down it was Jack. 'Jack… stop them… what's going on.'

'Don't worry Denise… he'll be fine… it's Ok.'

'But… but…'

'There you go again Denise… what did John say?'

'I'm not a goat…'

'Yes… let them do what they need to do… it will be Ok… honestly.'

The policemen looked at each other with their mouths wide open.

'Did that dog just talk? Am I hearing things?'

'I heard it too.'

'Yeah me too.'

'Something really strange is happening,' said the older policeman examining John's every move.

As everyone watched, John was completely engulfed by all the animals swirling around him and then he popped to the surface like a piece of wood floating in a stream. He was laid on his back with his arms outstretched and his body weight completely supported by all the animals beneath him. He glided along until he reached the Yew tree where they gently let him down and he sat crossed-legged, leaning forward slightly so his hands could reach the water. He looked up and smiled at Denise whose eyes instantly flooded with so many tears she had to wipe them from her face to see what was going on… she had a feeling in her stomach… but not a good one… the sort you get when you've just had terrible news and your stomach sinks.

'JOHN,' she called, stretching out a hand towards him, but he didn't reply.

Up until that moment the animals and birds, even the insects and bees had been as close to him as it was possible to get, but then John raised both his hands in the air which seemed to be a signal for them to leave and give him some space, because that's exactly what happened… they all moved back about two yards, standing and sitting motionless, and so quiet you could hear a mouse picking its nose.

John plunged his hands into the still water and lowered his head so his chin was touching his chest. He remained like that for about ten seconds… and then the water began to glow a golden yellow. The roots from the new tree must have been in the water because they started to take the water up into its trunk, branches, and finally the leaves, making the whole tree look like a road map of bright, golden roads linking all parts of the Yew tree together… it looked fantastic. The tree began to gleam and shine like the water, brighter and brighter until all of a sudden the dazzling light dimmed showing John beneath glowing just like the tree with all of his veins and arteries lit up as if they were full of liquid gold pumping through his body. Once again the glow emanating from John and the Yew tree began to increase, brighter and brighter, getting more and more intense until finally it was so bright it was impossible to distinguish John from the tree… all that was visible if you could look at it at all, was a bright white spot of light… like a star.

'What's happening?' Cried Carol shielding her eyes with her hands.

'I don't know Carol... I can't see,' replied Denise doing the same as she felt something moving between her ankles... it was Jack. She knelt down and pulled Jack close to hug her.

'It's getting brighter... too bright... aaaaaahhh,' screamed Carol and Denise in unison as the penetrating powerful white light engulfed them and everything around them...

Then, without warning... it exploded into a million smaller bright white stars which slowly sank to the ground and dissolved into nothing leaving John's body slumped head-first beneath the Yew tree.

'JOHN...' screamed Denise as she ran across the grass to where he was sitting leant forward face-down. 'John...'

But he didn't answer.

When she got within a few inches of him she stretched out her hand to touch him but she stopped... frozen for a second.

What if he was dead? He looked different... his hair was longer and darker... she couldn't see his hands because they were still in the water, so, slowly, she managed to find the courage to place her hand on his shoulder... he was hot to the touch, so hot, she recoiled her hand back in shock and when she looked closely there was steam coming from his body and the top of his head. She grabbed his shoulder again and quickly yanked his body back letting go as soon as he began to topple backwards, so as not to burn her hand. She gently pushed him to one side so he landed on his side on the grass with his legs stretched out.

She dropped down onto her knees beside him and immediately knew there was something wrong because his face was distorted and unrecognisable, almost grotesque. She cupped her hands over her face and leaned forward until her forehead touched the grass, sobbing.

'John... John... John...' she kept repeating his name as tears streamed down her face which seeped between her fingers and dripped to the ground. She sat back slightly, and with tear-soaked hands, she put one on each of his contorted cheeks. The moment she touched his face, his skin sizzled like dropping vinegar onto limestone. She rapidly drew her hands back and could see that where she had touched his skin, it had peeled away and underneath she could see fresh pink skin. Carefully she touched his face and it sizzled again exposing fresh skin, so she gently rubbed her hands all over his face and neck removing the peeling top layer to reveal the John she knew… but more than that… a much younger John.

He was handsome. She had never noticed that before. Yes, she had noticed he was quite good-looking, but now she saw how handsome he really was.

She leaned forward and gently kissed him on his lips.

The moment her lips touched his, he took a sharp intake of breath and his eyes slowly opened.

'Mmm…' He whispered fixing his eyes with hers. 'What a beautiful thing to wake up to.'

She laughed out loud as tears rolled down her face and she began to hug him harder than she had ever hugged anyone before.

'Careful.' He said with a huge smile on his face. 'You don't want to break me.'

'Err… excuse me,' came a voice from behind Denise as she knelt next to John who was now sitting up.

'I recognise that voice,' said John slowly getting to his feet. 'Jack… how are you?'

'How am I… you old fool… how are you?'

'I'm good,' John replied putting his arm around Denise's shoulder. 'Really good.'

'We all thought we'd lost you then,' said Jack turning his head slightly to gesture around him at all the animals that had now come back much closer and were all gathered around.

'Promise us John... you won't do that again... ever.'

'Not if I can help it I won't,' He replied loudly directing his answer to the thousands and thousands of nature's creatures gathered around him, who on hearing his reply all roared, squeaked, tweeted, bellowed, and whatever other noises they make, at the top of their voices, so loud it could be heard from the main street of the village two hundred yards away.

All the time this had been going on, from the moment John put his hands into the water, the light shining through him and his rebirth, the four policemen and Carol had been watching in stunned silence with their mouths wide open in amazement.

'I cannot believe what we have just witnessed,' said Carol as she made her way through the mass of animals to where John and Denise were now standing hand in hand. 'It was amazing... fantastic... a miracle.'

'You see Carol... I told you this place was special,' Denise replied slipping her hand around John's waist and smiling up at him.

'Special is not the word... I have to get this in the paper... although no one will believe me.'

'Err... Carol is it?' Interrupted one of the younger policemen. 'I recorded everything on my phone... look.' He strode over to them, carefully avoiding the animals, and began to find the recording... but to everyone's amazement, the only thing it recorded was an intense bright light... nothing else. 'Oh... bugger... I don't know what went wrong. Let me take a quick recording now,' he said pointing his camera at John and Denise for a few seconds to get a recording. When he replayed it, Denise was shown OK but there was an intense white light in the centre of John which obliterated him completely. 'I don't understand it.'

'I think I do... Let me try,' Said Carol pointing her phone at John and Denise and recording for a few seconds. When she played it back it was identical to the policeman's recording... the middle of John's body was lit up like a brilliant shimmering star.

'I don't know what's going on... but whatever it is... it's important," said Carol looking at her phone and then at John.

'Carol, when you write about this will you please tell the developers not to build here?' pleaded Denise.

'Of course... how can anyone build here... it's a miracle... in fact more than one miracle has happened here... this place is special... REALLY special... just like you John.'

***

Time has passed but Beckside is still there, almost completely hidden away in a quiet part of Appleton Roebuck, and no one has built on the field... Yet.

It's still a haven for many different types of animals ranging from the smallest vole to the largest deer and if you're lucky, if you're *very* lucky, and can sneak a peek through the trees from the track, you might just catch a glimpse of John working on his land with Jack by his side, occasionally stopping to chat with one of his animal or bird friends... and who knows, you might just get to see him or one of his little friends drink from the incredible golden pond under the Yew tree.

The End... for now